W9-CCS-091

PRAISE FOR LOCAL STAR

"*Local Star* is a heartfelt, heartwarming polyam romance driven by mystery, intrigue, and action, whose grease-stained main character works to repair more than just ships. Ogden assembles a universe of complex people and problems, then drills down to a story about love, family, self-acceptance, and forgiveness."

—VALERIE VALDES, AUTHOR OF *CHILLING EFFECT*

"A smart, witty exploration of what it means to be a family, *Local Star* combines the thoughtful humanism of *A Closed and Common Orbit* with a delightfully quirky setting reminiscent of the best works of Bruce Sterling.

For years now, members of the SFF community have known that Aimee Ogden is a writer who can be counted on to deliver insightful stories packed with beautiful, flowing prose. The day after this book is published, everyone will know."

—ROBYN BENNIS, AUTHOR OF *THE GUNS ABOVE*

"I pick up everything I see with Ogden's name on it and I am never disappointed! *Local Star* sits in that lovely intersection of the personal and the operatic, hinting at intergalactic-level conflict while remaining deeply wedded to the life and loves of its heroine—a former guttergirl-turned-ship-mechanic who doesn't meet a problem she can't barrel through. Sweet and romantic. Highly recommended!"

SAMANTHA MILLS, SHORT FICTION AUTHOR

"In navigating familial ties amidst a backdrop of war, Triz carves out a space in a queer community that, despite its far-flung location, rings familiar and true. A dazzling tale of interstellar intrigue, *Local Star* is beautiful contemplation on what it means to be a family."

SUZANNE WALKER, CO-CREATOR OF THE HUGO-NOMINATED GRAPHIC NOVEL *MOONCAKES* WITH ARTIST WENDY XU

ALSO BY AIMEE OGDEN

Sun-Daughters, Sea Daughters (2021) from *Tor.com*

"A Song for the Leadwood Tree" in *Beneath Ceaseless Skies*

"His Heart is the Haunted House" in *Apparition Lit*

"Seb Dreams of Reincarnation" in *Escape Pod*

"Shelter, Sustenance, Self" in *Fireside*

This is a work of fiction. All of the characters, organizations, and events portrayed are either products of the author's imagination or used fictitiously.

LOCAL STAR

Copyright © 2020 by Aimee Ogden.

All rights reserved.

No part of this book may be reproduced in any form or by any electronic or mechanical means, including information storage and retrieval systems, without written permission from the author and publisher, except for the use of brief quotations in a book review.

Cover illustration by Oleg Tsoy.

Edited by Holly Lyn Walrath.

Published by Interstellar Flight Press, Houston, Texas.

www.interstellarflightpress.com

ISBN (eBook): 978-1-953736-00-0

ISBN (Paperback): 978-1-953736-02-4

First Edition: 2021

LOCAL STAR

AIMEE OGDEN

INTERSTELLAR FLIGHT PRESS

CHAPTER ONE

NORMALLY, there was nowhere Triz Cierrond would rather be than elbows-deep in a starfighter. But twenty levels above her, the Hab's main Arcade was crammed with people celebrating the victorious return of the Confederated Fleet. For once in her life, the station wrenchworks were the last place she wanted to be.

And Kalo was the last person she wanted to be stuck there with.

It was partly her fault for making him wait while she finished checking the other six light attack Swarmers. But if she had to be miserable, her ex might as well be too. Soon, *soon*, she'd be uphab celebrating with Casne and her quadparents. A small part of her knew she was hesitating over that too. Probably best to wait a few hours anyway, to give them some time to try being one big happy family. She still didn't know how she fit into that equation.

Triz ducked under the left-hand engine pod of Kalo's swarmer, noting an oozing coolant leak where the wing had partially sheared away from the fuselage. Scorch marks streaked the cockpit, and the nosecone was less of a cone now than an impact-flattened nub. She shook her head and recorded a note on the tablet: *total wrench job.* "Shitting stars," she muttered, and pulled her facemask up over her nose and mouth. "How are you not dead after this?"

"I apologize on behalf of the Cyberbionautic Alliance. I'm sure the Ceebees wish they'd finished the job almost as much as you do." Kalo sprawled atop Triz's eternally-in-progress refit of an Escoth V-27 engine assembly. The Escoth, as well as the pile of damaged ore-Scoopers hurriedly rearranged behind it, had been set aside for the sudden influx of paying work. Ships like Escoths were fast and sporty, great for fixing up and selling for a little credit. The Scoopers were scavenger crafts that filtered through the silt layers on the outside of asteroids, panning for something richer than iron oxide in that dust. Kalo didn't seem to mind his precarious position. If the prospect of getting oil on his dress greens alarmed him, he didn't show it. He didn't look at her but combed one hand through wavy, dark hair. He needed a haircut.

Not that it mattered much how he looked. Once he escaped to the festivities uphab, he and anyone else in a Fleet uniform would be deluged by offers of drinks and dalliances tonight, and those with a Light Attack Swarm pin on their collar more than most. Greaseball mechanics just didn't invite the same level of attention—especially the ones who'd grown up as guttergirls in a recycling engine, with the manners to match.

Casne would probably be just as beset with admirers as Kalo . . . but Triz knew her best friend and most significant of others wouldn't be entertaining outside interest tonight.

Some things were worth waiting for. Triz dragged her stylus across the screen of her tablet, scratching out her notes one slow stroke at a time. She glanced over at Kalo, who was fidgeting with one of his silver-ringed cuffs. Good. Let him be impatient.

"I was thinking," said Kalo, and Triz's stylus froze against the screen. There were a lot of things that could come after those three words, and she doubted any of them would improve the current situation. "The atmospheric handling hasn't been great for me lately. The greaseheads over at Auzhni Hab got a little creative with the repairs after that little to-do outside Hedgehome, and it's not exactly sticking on a hard turn, but it's not exactly *not*, either. If you could just get in there and change the calibration of the—"

"Don't tell me how to do my job." She scratched off the rest of the note in shorthand, signed it, and stormed across the wrenchworks bay to thrust the tablet at Kalo. "It'll take me forever to get this thing spaceworthy. How long is the Fleet here?" Longer meant more time with Casne; it also meant more chances for head-to-head collisions with Kalo and the shrapnel of their former relationship.

It was supposed to be fun. *Kalo* was supposed to be fun. Until he'd neatly snipped things off right before the Fleet left for Hedgehome: no reasons, just a polite this-isn't-working-is-it, just shy of nine cycles after Casne had enthusiastically introduced them—almost a whole year together, reckoning by the local star. But no great surprise there: they'd been skimming that event horizon for a while already. Triz had found herself starting idle fights whenever Kalo was back on-Hab, finding annoyances in little things that hadn't bothered her before. They'd had a screaming fight when the Hab got 'port footage of the destruction of the CFS Graithe and the

Iuelo outside Ceebee territory. Just as well he'd ended things not long after that, because gods, was it annoying to ask someone to give a shit about you as they flew blithely off to their untimely death!

At least Casne crewed a whaleship, one of those practically Hab-sized behemoths with just enough engines attached to nudge them through space. Whaleships were built to withstand fire, cradling their heavy-fire tactical arrays, providing a safe haven for their battered swarms to return to after battle. Whaleships always came home . . . almost always. With Light Attack Swarms, the odds weren't so good. And when they did come home, it might well be in pieces of a size suitable for packing in a mealcase.

He'd left her. And now he was back here, in her 'works. Trying to be *friendly*. If Kalo noticed her taut silence while scanning through her notes, he didn't reach out to strum it. He scrolled upward several times to get through her full report, and he whistled low when he reached the end. "Gods of Issam. I really should be dead."

"Better luck next time." She poked his hand that held the stylus, and he dashed off a signature. The tablet chirped politely, and an invoice estimate winged its way to the Fleet bursary at Centerpoint. "Maybe next time, don't burn so hard on a wing you know is busted."

"Don't tell *me* how to do my job." Kalo tossed the tablet back to her, and she caught it low, just a few inches above the ground. "Thanks for the lookover. The Fleet's parked here for three days while we refuel and wait for Centerpoint to stop shitting their pants over what to do with the Ceebees and actually send usf new orders. If you don't have the time to fix me up altogether, at least get things started so the techs on the whaleship don't have to start from scratch." His mouth twisted in that familiar half-smile she couldn't help but love to hate. "Or if you're short on time, you can skip making it spaceworthy and just set up a feedback loop in the coolant line so I blow up halfway between here and Centerpoint. That'll save both you and the techs a lot of trouble."

"I wouldn't." Dragging a clearance hose, she retreated back under the Swarmer, as much to put some space between them as to start working. "Casne would know it was me, and I'd never hear the end of it."

He followed her over to the repair bay and leaned against the good wing with one arm. "Well, I certainly wouldn't want my murder to cause you any inconvenience. Besides, you'd miss me if I was space dust."

The hose was heavy; Triz bent her knees to get under it and tried not to look like she was struggling. He might do something really hideous, like offer to help. "The only way I'd miss you is with a lancet gun. And not more than once."

He ducked his head under the fuselage. "And yet here we are, alone in the wrenchworks. By your plan, by the way, not mine. Not that I'm objecting. If there's anything you wanted to say—"

The metallorganic seal on the hose suctioned itself onto the gaping wound in the side of Kalo's Swarmer, and Triz flipped the switch on the pump with her foot. The vacuum clattered twice then roared to life, slurping down the coolant spillage and its unwanted fumes. "We're all set here," Triz shouted over the noisy belching of the pump. She wasn't sure if Kalo could hear her over the noise and didn't especially care. The vacuum spoke for itself.

He yelled something back at her and gestured to the pair of lifts that stretched through the Hab. The wrenchworks made up the bottom of the station—or at least what everyone agreed via the consensus of artificial gravity counted as "bottom," in deep space—and the lift started here, then crossed the recycling and recovery levels, the living quarters, and the Arcade, ending in Justice at the very top. Maybe he was asking where to go now? Triz couldn't pick just *one* of the seven hells, so she shrugged and slipped her earmuffs from around her neck to cover her ears. Finally, Kalo gave up and disappeared into one of the lifts.

Triz gave it two minutes to make sure he was really gone, then collapsed against the battered Swarmer. Intellectually, she knew the fighting between the Ceebees and the Confederated Fleet had been ugly. She'd seen the vids of dead alien intelligences after the Ceebee commander's attempts at rapidfire terraforming: lifeless mounds of iridescent tendrils and broken segments of carapace, poisoned by the introduction of atmospheric oxygen. Sitting beside the newsport, she'd listened to the rolls of names of planetary colonists killed in the forcible resettlements at Hedgehome. Ceebees never balked at remaking their own bodies, using any and every tech available to fit themselves to their environment; they'd proven they had equally few qualms about remaking an environment to better serve them—to often horrific effect.

It was strange now, to have the war brought to her own door like this. Usually, the wrenchworks here at her home habitation ring of Vivik didn't see more than the odd freighter every week or two. Vivik's local star had no habitable planets and nothing particular to recommend it beyond a gas giant resort for platform jumpers. Even its economic role as a shipping-lane nexus for the past hundred years only allowed freight to pass through on its way to the bigger systems farther out.

Triz liked Vivik Hab's usual quiet. Her home for the past

ten years had always offered her safety. But Moxu and Vogett, the two closest big Habs on this ragged edge of settled space, had been destroyed in the fighting, leaving Vivik the only nearby survivor able to pick up the pieces of the Fleet and send it on to the center of the Galactic Web. Ships weren't the only wreckage clotting the Hab. None other than Commander Rocan shitting Dustald-3 Melviq himself was a prisoner of Justice here. Many of Vivik's citizens had already gone to war; now war had come to the Hab itself.

When she could breathe again, she emerged from under the Swarmer's belly and hurried into the wrenchworks office. The earmuffs clanged when she tossed them into her locker, and she scanned her wristfob for a tiny water ration to splash her face in the sink. She didn't want to open the fighter up until she was sure it was coolant-free, so no reason not to celebrate with the rest of the Hab. She could buy a round for some friendly-looking whaleship crews and still give Casne time and space to enjoy her quadparents for a while yet.

No time to bother with changing into something fancier; Triz ducked out of the office and fussed briefly with her hair. She wondered if she'd be able to find any of Casne's Fleet friends to follow around for the night. If nothing else, she might be able to find them on the outskirts of the crowd of admirers the favored Captain Casne Vivik Veling had surely collected by now. They could hit Ganit's Pantry, and hopefully Ganit hadn't jacked up the price of boot gin by three hundred percent for the night—

The lift flashed an alert: visitors incoming. Damn Kalo. What, did he decide to give it one more go for old time's sake? Her heart lurched. But then a comfortably familiar scowl settled into her face, and she folded her arms.

The lift doors parted, and Triz choked on the deep breath she'd held. Casne exploded out of the lift and picked her up in a hug. Triz's arms locked around Casne's back, and she gasped down a deep breath to keep from bursting into sudden, silly tears. Casne's tight curls carried the faint electric smell of the interior of a whaleship, but she still smelled like home to Triz.

After several long moments that would never be quite long enough, Casne pulled back. "All right, greasemark," she shouted over the vacuum's roaring and laid a warm kiss on Triz's lower lip. "Are you going to buy me a drink, or what?"

CHAPTER TWO

THE LIFT MOVED TOO FAST: up through Metal Reclamation and the Terraria level that served as the Hab's living lungs, through the umbilicus ring where Fleet ships trailed on the ends of their leads, then layers and layers of living quarters. After a too-short minute's frantic reacquaintance behind the closed lift doors, Casne and Triz were deposited at the top end of the Hab in the middle of an utterly unrecognizable Arcade. Gray and gold streamers spanned the space between the central lift column and the businesses that wrapped around the station perimeter. Some of them were proper custom-printed decorations, while others had been hastily assembled from paper scraps or mealcase wrappers. The decor closed in the wide-open Arcade, made it feel smaller, more enclosed, despite the windows all around that peered out into the open void of space.

Triz recoiled from the sight of all that empty black, chopped up into tiny pieces as it was by the myriad of windows lining the Arcade. In one corner of the window, over the main recycling chute, a small arc of the local star could be seen—a glimmer of gold against the darkness. All the orange dwarf's planets were tidally locked and uninhabitable, so the Hab's solar arrays had been built to take advantage of the otherwise-unused light and heat.

Triz appreciated the change in the Arcade's atmosphere, but she paused a moment in the frame of the lift doors. That was a lot of people. A lot of noise, a lot of *everything*. Not many folks here had ever recoiled from her as if she still reeked of recycling engine—and she suspected Casne had sorted those out long ago. People here didn't remember her as the guttergirl she'd grown up as back on Rydoine. Still. She couldn't shake the sense she didn't totally belong here, in this world of smiles and songs and light.

Casne smoothed Triz's hair back from her forehead. "Come on, guttergirl," Casne said, "you're with me now," and Triz took a deep breath as they careened out into the crowd.

They leaned into one another to stay together in the press of bodies, tripping over other people's feet as well as the occasional empty moonshine bottle.

"Your dad must have given PubWel a break," Triz shouted over the crowd. PubWel, the monitors of public welfare, must be politely looking the other way tonight. Or possibly they were at the bottom of another bottle themselves, instead of spending the celebratory night politely realigning the Hab to the norms of perfect eusocial behavior.

Casne's laugh rolled warmly down Triz's cheek. "Quelian just *wishes* he got to run public welfare like it's part of his wrenchworks, but that's not exactly how it goes, you know. He's a civilian tribune, not the god of Justice."

"I still don't think he'll be doing much to tamp down on tonight's activities. Nothing like having your prodigal daughter return in star-studded glory to convince a man that maybe she's done all right for herself after all."

At that, Casne only grunted. Triz knew Quelian had been upset when Casne ran off to join the Fleet. But she couldn't imagine how he could hang on to that old anger now, with all Casne had done. She let the subject slide and ducked her head into Casne's shoulder to avoid the spray from a freshly popped bottle of fizzy-slosh. At Casne's squawk of dismay, she cackled a laugh. In answer, Casne picked Triz up around the waist and wiped her wet, sticky face off on Triz's already-mussed worksuit, ignoring Triz's squalls of protest. Together they staggered, shrieking with laughter, into the minilift doors as they opened. Triz stepped on someone's foot—not Casne's.

Triz turned and looked up into Quelian's dubious face.

"Baba!" Casne said to her father, reaching uncharacteristic heights of joviality before Triz could croak an apology. "We were just talking about you."

"I got all the Swarmers inventoried," Triz cut in, crushing a foot—Casne's—on purpose this time. "Started drainage on the worst one and started two batches of algae cultures incubating, so they'll be ready for you first thing in the morning."

"Ready for me?" Quelian's frown didn't deepen, exactly, only shifted somehow. He was much fairer than Casne, whose looks took more after her mother, but there was a certain . . . stubbornness these two shared. When Casne and Triz were teens, he'd taken on a role as one of the habitation ring's tribunes, expecting to transition away from the wrenchworks entirely once Casne came of age to take over.

Then she'd gone and run off to be a Fleetie. Overworked and overtired as he was these days, he didn't seem quite as eager, somehow, to hand off the 'works to his daughter's guttergirl-partner. "I assume you'll be in somewhat later than *first thing* yourself?"

"Baba." Casne's perfectly cheerful tone sheathed steel. "Has Triz ever slacked off a day in her life?" She pursed her lips. "Where are Daddy and Damu and Mama?"

"I queued up to handle the tab while the others took your mother home." Now a touch of humor tugged at his mouth. "She drank enough brandy tonight to drop a Tolvian martyr."

A flicker of guilt over missing time with Casne's family made Triz's shoulderblades jump. They got to see Triz plenty, more than they wanted, probably; better to let them have their one-on-one time with Cas.

"In fact, it's probably just as well you excused yourself when you did," Quelian went on. "All three of them send their regards, Triz. Veling said to remind you that you're invited to dinner tomorrow night."

These "family" dinners hadn't stopped, as Triz had half-expected, when the quadfamily's only daughter had gone off to war. Having grown up a guttergirl in another Hab's recycling engines, Triz found any meal she didn't have to fight for to be a gift; she was embarrassed and pleased to still be included when she was outside of Casne's shadow.

They wanted her to be a part of their extended family, so why was Triz so hesitant?

Quelian looked between Triz and Casne once more and sighed, looking not a little martyr-ish himself. "Enjoy yourselves, then. I'm sure you will." He shouldered his way out into the Arcade crowds as others finally nudged Triz and Casne forward and into the minilift.

"Gods," said Casne, and sighed. "I don't know why I'm surprised. You know how he is."

Triz did know. After Casne had first invited Triz to join her and her wife Nantha in their marriage, Triz had tried calling Quelian 'baba' too. *Once.* The look he'd given her could've slagged plastiglass. "Didn't your parents want to see you tonight?" she asked, now that Quelian's dour mood had kindled a trashfire of guilt in her belly.

"Trying to get rid of me already?" Casne's elbow dug into Triz's ribs as the minilift spat them out on the second level of the Arcade, where most of the eateries and, more importantly, *drinkeries* were located. "They were waiting for me as soon as I offloaded. We had dinner while you were slumming it in the wrenchworks. Which, by the way . . . *why* were you doing that exactly? Mama told me she couldn't dislodge you out of there with a crowbar and a bottle of brandy. Wasn't the same without all six of us together. We even had Nantha on the 'port."

A flush crept up Triz's neck, and she let a little space come between her body and Casne's. It was always nice when Casne talked about her like she was really one of them, and still awkward too, because she *wasn't.* "I wish Nan could've been here too. To celebrate all together."

"Nan said the same thing." Casne arched an eyebrow. "But I bet if Fleet Admiralty tried to unplug her from her calculation matrices right now, she'd claw her way right back into them. With those three inbound deployments, the navigators are up to their necks in math about now and she *lives* for that stuff."

"Says the Tactics number-jockey." They both laughed,

and Triz ducked her head in embarrassment. "Anyway, your parents deserved to have you to themselves."

"Well, you're basically part of the family. More than basically, if you ever get around to formalizing it, which by the way, Nantha and I are *still* waiting for you to say yes to." A snort. "Besides, if you'd been there, maybe Mama wouldn't have done so much damage to the brandy on her own. Oh!" Casne let her hand slide down Triz's arm until they only clasped fingers so they could slide one after the other through a flock of Fleet engineers and their admirers. "Speaking of the wrenchworks. That must have been Kalo's Swarmer on the blocks down there? Did the Hero of Hedgehome tell you about how he took out an entire Ceebee orbital installation on one good engine?" She laughed, and the sweet sound drew Triz in close again. "I guess not, seeing as you're not still down there getting your ear bent."

Not this again. Triz grimaced. "Kalo and I don't have a lot to say to each other these days. Shitting stars, Cas, you know that." It had been Casne who introduced her to Kalo. Triz knew just how much Casne wanted them to hit it off, wanted them to have a gon.

"Well, yeah. But Nantha and I always thought . . ." Casne pulled Triz into the shuttered doorway of the bakery. "He hasn't told me what happened between you two yet, either."

Triz raised her eyebrows into Casne's expectant silence. "Okay? You know I don't care if you keep sleeping with him. I don't even care if you want to bring him into your gon instead of me."

"Triz." Casne grimaced at the magnitude of that lie. "You know you don't have to wait till you find a fourth, right? We love you and we want *you* to be part of our gon. I know you like the idea of a quad but a triad is a good start. Or finish, for that matter. Now, later. Whenever."

"I know that." Triz rested her forehead against Casne's strong shoulder. It felt good, and she didn't have to meet Cas' eyes. She knew Casne and Nantha both cared for her, that whatever triad or quad or pent they ended up with would be a beautiful thing. And she also knew Casne and Nantha had been together for about a million turns, and as a triad, they would be Casne and Nantha (and Triz), not Casne and Nantha and Triz, and she wanted a partner of her own to bring to that table. Both so she wouldn't feel that tiny bit of extra distance, and so Casne and Nantha wouldn't realize it was there and feel guilty about it. They would always have their own history from before Triz, their private, personal language of Academy stresses and first Fleet assignments that Triz had learned to understand but never to speak. Some people were suns, some were moons, and some were just rocks who soaked up others' light and warmth. Triz was not a sun.

"All right. As long as you know." Casne rocked a bit from side to side, making Triz dance with her. "So do you want me to throw someone at you? Not another Fleetie then, but—"

Triz's face scrunched up; she pulled back a bit to frown up at Casne. "Why would I care if it's someone from the Fleet?"

"I thought that's why you and Kalo—never mind."

She hated how well Casne knew her, and she loved it too.

"Well, do you want me and Nan to ruminate on that one?"

"No! I mean, maybe. I don't . . ." Triz sighed and rolled her face to the side. Her forehead found the damp heat of

Casne's neck. "I just need time to—to figure things out. All right?"

"Sure. Yes. Sorry." Casne rolled them side-by-side back into the cheerful fracas of the Arcade; her arm lingered around Triz's neck. "Let's just have fun tonight. You remember my friends Lanniq and Saabe, right?"

"Of course!" Triz liked getting to spend time with Casne's Fleet friends. A little glimpse of life out there in the black, without the unpleasant necessity of actually having to put a Hab behind her. At fifteen, she'd been rescued (though broadly speaking, proper rescues surely involved less screaming and biting on behalf of the rescued) from the bottom of Rydoine Hab, crammed into a spaceship, and pitched out into the void. No more dark familiar recycling caves, only the endless black, swallowing her alive. In her panic to get back, she'd managed to scratch a plastiglass viewport on the ship the Tolvian mendicants had chartered across the Galactic Web from Rydoine to Vivik. Even the other gutterkids had been a little scared of her, then.

"Great!" Casne pulled her around the bend of the Arcade. "They're at Edillo's. Come on!"

"Edillo's," Triz echoed.

Hopefully, she'd changed enough since her guttergirl days not to embarrass Casne and her Fleetie friends in an upclass joint like that. "Okay. I'll buy the first round."

* * *

THE STEWARD at Edillo's had given up on his usual hospitality rituals; he couldn't even contrive to pour drinks himself for the crowd of Fleet uniforms invading the normally quiet lounge. Instead, he sold Triz two bottles of spicewine at a severe markup while he hunched over the opening of his stock cubby. "Glasses?" she shouted over the background din, but he had already turned away to a pair of ensigns who were trying to open the taps drilled into the gnarled moonshine tree that formed the centerpiece of the establishment. When the steward cornered the ensigns and launched into a tirade about the history of the tree and the great-grandmothers who had planted it, Triz gave up. She retreated through the crush of bodies to the pile of cushions in the back corner where Casne's friends had staked out space.

Casne's fellow captain, Lanniq Erron-2 Kett, was the most beautiful man Triz had ever met. His skin was a few shades lighter than Casne's, and like her, he wore his hair shaved down close. His shoulders and waist formed very nearly a perfect triangle, and Triz found herself staring more than once while he recounted heroics from the battle at Golros. Too bad he was already firmly ensconced in a stable triad of his own, or Triz might've made a play for him. When he leaned in to take the spicewine out of Triz's hand, his fingers were warm against hers, and he flashed her a lopsided smile. Maybe she'd make a play for him anyway, especially if Casne was too tired to come back to Triz's place tonight. One small catch: he was a Light Attack pilot. But one night wasn't a gon and after all, Triz told herself, no one was *perfect.*

Then again . . . his smile had dropped off his face, even before he had the spicewine open. Triz remembered Casne had told her not to bring up his family tonight—something about his nephew falling in with the Ceebees, with no word from him since the battle at Hedgehome. That sounded like the kind of thing that would severely overshadow even a ringing victory like the one the Fleet just enjoyed.

"We were just getting to the good part," Lanniq said, by way of greeting. He got the sealer off the wine and drank a mouthful. No one asked about the missing cups. "But I don't tell it as well as Kalo. Where is he?"

"You don't tell it as well as Kalo because you don't do the sound effects. You gotta do the sound effects." Saabe, a lanky lieutenant from the low-grav colony on Andeus, leaned in to reach for the wine bottle. E took a deep swig and gargled it violently, miming with eir arms a starfighter in flight. Casne elbowed em hard, making the bottle jump in eir hand; Lanniq rescued it and Saabe sat back, chagrined. "Anyway, old Pokey is probably spilling his heroic saga to the poor greasemark stuck with him in the wrenchworks. Maybe making time with them, too, if he's lucky. He's been churning heavy atmo since before Hedgehome, poor guy."

Triz stiffened. "Looked to me like the only thing spilling in the works was the entire flight assembly of 'Pokey's' Skimmer. Do you cockpit jockeys know you don't win a fight by collecting the most shrapnel with your fuselage?"

"Lieutenant," Casne said, a little louder than was necessary to cut through the background chatter. Saabe's spine straightened as if by instinct. "Do you remember my partner Triz, who works? For my father? In the Vivik wrenchworks?"

"Oh! Shitting stars." Saabe scrambled to make room on the cushions for Triz to slide in between em and Casne. "I didn't recognize you without your, I mean, when you're not —you and Kalo were, uh." E jumped when Casne cuffed em amicably on the back of the head. "Sorry."

"It's nothing. Just pass the wine."

She'd just raised the bottle to her lips when a four-note fanfare played over the bar's speakers. The strangely upbeat tone covered the lowkey rhythm of the music beating a moment before, and the lights flashed on and off to match the beat. She didn't recognize it as one of the Hab's alarm codes. She took a big gulp before noticing the three Fleet officers around her had gone stiff. "What does that mean? What's going on?"

"It's him," said Casne, standing. She waited just long enough for Triz to catch up before shoving through the throng of patrons who now crowded toward the door out onto the Arcade.

Thanks to Casne's imposing figure, they made their way up to the railing that looked down into the lower levels. A moment later, both Saabe and Lanniq butted up against them. Triz wanted to ask again exactly what was going on, and whether they were likely to lose their prime seats in Edillo's by the time all this was over, but clamped her mouth shut when the main lift doors below opened. The quiet swarms of revelers pushed back from the doors as a quartet of Fleet officers emerged. They must have boarded the Hab several levels down, at the umbilicus band. The Hab lights glared on their helmets' visors, lending an eerie sheen of sameness to the group; on each shoulder, they bore the insignia of their home whaleship. From here, Triz couldn't make out which it was; she didn't think it was Casne's home ship, the Dailos. When she turned to ask Casne, the hard look on her face stopped her short.

More movement drew her eye back down. Another figure emerged from the lift, and behind him, four more guards. Only the man in the middle had his helmet off, and Triz gasped when she recognized him. "That's *him*," she said. "That's Rocan Melviq."

"The one and only Lord Commander," said Lanniq, as Saabe muttered, "He's just a figurehead."

More theories came jumbling out of the two of them. "My cousin whose ex-partner works for Fleet Intelligence says the Ceebees still have another secret terraforming project underway," Saabe said.

"No." Lanniq's hands tightened on the railing in front of him. "They're done for after Hedgehome and Chimon. The tide of this war has turned. I believe that." He said it like a man who needed to believe it. Triz wondered again about the nephew who'd disappeared. Would he come slinking home now that the Ceebees had been routed, or was he on his way home already in a Fleet prison cell?

Saabe clucked and shook eir head. "That's what they want us to think. But I'll bet you a month's sugar rations that they still have reserves hidden out there. Maybe somewhere webward of Golros . . ."

Triz gave up on following the argument and returned to Casne's side. When her hand brushing Casne's arm didn't dislodge her viselike grip on the railing, she prized Casne's fingers up and clasped them herself instead. Casne squeezed once, then relaxed. "Look at him, Triz. He's enjoying it."

Casne was right. As the anonymous Fleet officers marched Rocan forward, hissed curses and whispered disgust followed them. The Ceebee Commander wore a small, calm smile. "They're taking him to Justice?" Triz asked, as his escorts directed him into the minilift. A bottle smashed against the doors just as they closed; a Hab security guard with his uniform jacket hanging open half-heartedly pushed his way through the crowd while a trio of cleanerbots zipped between legs to take care of the broken glass. "Why march him through the Arcade in the middle of the party? They should have at least left his helmet on."

"Civilians love a show," said Casne grimly. Her expression thawed slightly. "Sorry."

Triz wondered if they'd sentence him to cryo until the hearings started. Practically a death sentence for a man who, rumor said, had bioengineered away his need for sleep. She shifted from foot to foot. "As long as this is the beginning of the end for the Ceebees." She craned her neck as though she could see through the Arcade's ceiling into Justice. "There's something wrong with them. I mean, they think they're entitled to wipe entire worlds and terraform them for their own use . . . Something about what they do to themselves must mess them up in the head. I can't understand why anyone would want to mod their perfectly good body that way."

When Triz turned to the others, Lanniq was grimacing down at his own boots. Casne's mouth opened, then closed, then opened again, then opened for a splash of the spicewine she'd had stashed under her arm. When she spoke, the wine roughened her voice. "Triz, you had your eyes done three years ago to fix your myopia. And what about Nantha's reassignment?"

"That's not the same thing at all!" Triz protested. "Ceebees are more machine than human."

"Are you saying you think that anyone with mods—" Casne closed her eyes for a moment, then shook her head. "No. Let's not. We're here to celebrate, not fight."

Lanniq cleared his throat. The crowds had begun to flow back in the directions of the eateries and bars and tea rooms. "I'm going to go save our table. You all coming?"

"I definitely am," Saabe sighed. "The artigrav on this Hab is too shitting high, I need to sit down again."

Triz peeled off from the group as they squeezed through the doorway of the bar. "I'll get another bottle," she said.

Obviously, she'd ruffled feathers, but maybe she could smooth them down again if she poured enough spicewine on.

"You sure?" Casne plucked at her sleeve. "Is Quelian paying you so much you can afford to keep three Fleeties in booze all night?"

"I said another bottle, not all night." Triz laughed, and Casne let her break free with a lopsided grin. She looked around; the steward was nowhere to be seen, but a small crowd packed in around the door to Edillo's storage rooms. Triz edged forward and wedged herself in between a pair of bodies. "Excuse me," she mumbled, as the Fleet officer she'd bumped turned to face her.

It was Kalo, because of course it was Kalo. He was embedded in among a knot of Fleet folk, with a few civilian hangers-on mixed into the mess. When he saw her squeezed in next to him, his face folded into an embarrassed smirk, and he raised a glass of something smoky-green. Shitting stars. Not for the first time, she wished he wasn't so easy to look at. Wavy black hair, sleepy dark eyes, and crooked front teeth, just so he didn't look quite too pretty to be real. "Make yourself at home. What're you drinking?"

"Poison, with any luck."

His gaze flicked to Casne and her other Fleet friends in the corner, then back to Triz. "To your health, then." He slugged the smoky-green drink and turned into the crowd of Fleeties and civilians packed around him.

Triz managed to flag down the steward and swapped a fob-scan for a bottle of Simek green wine: decidedly a lesser vintage than the first round. The steward got an earful of Triz's disapproval, mostly because she was annoyed Kalo had somehow scored actual drinking glasses while she was stuck drinking from the bottle like a slob. She slouched back toward the cushioned corner with her second-rate prize tucked inside her elbow.

If the reduction in beverage quality disappointed anyone, they didn't mention it. Whatever awkwardness Triz had woken on the Arcade washed away under a sticky-sweet green tide. By the time the bottle had run dry, Triz was laughing herself sick over Saabe's story about how e had tried to smuggle Roian leather out of a planetary Arcology only to discover e had bought a living, oozing, two-foot-long Roian hideslug.

"I'm wiped," said Casne in Triz's ear, once she could breathe normally instead of whooping for air. "I'm ready to head back to your place. How much longer do you want to stay?"

Triz leaned into Casne, turning a private word into a kiss on the back of her neck. "My place? Oh, are you not heading back to the quadhome?" That got her a rude noise in response, and she hid a smile against her sleeve. "Then let's get out of here."

They bid goodnight to Lanniq, and Saabe, who wore a knowing grin of eir own, and stumbled out of the still-packed bar and onto the Arcade. Triz still had a half-bottle of green wine in one hand, but no one waited at the door to scold her for breaking flammable liquid regulations tonight. The air out here was cooler and fresher, and Triz gulped down a welcome breath in the hope it would sober her up a bit. She wanted to remember this tomorrow and the next day—and the next and the next. Casne slung an arm around her neck, and her brandy-scented sigh roll hot and wet down the side of Triz's cheek, and Triz thought sobriety might not be all it was cracked up to be.

"Captain Casne Vivik Veling?"

Heads cracked together, Triz's temple to Casne's chin, as they turned to take in whatever sycophant wanted a photo-snap or an autograph. A pair of uniforms stood side-by-side under the Arcade's bright lights. "Some other time," Triz said, but when she went to tug on Casne's arm, it had gone stiff inside her sleeve.

"Officers." Casne sounded cool and formal in a way she never did with Lanniq and Saabe, who were officers too, after all. Triz looked at these two again and noticed their uniforms, though cut to Fleet standard, were a pale brown color rather than the casual gray Casne wore. "How can I help you?"

The taller of the two, with a female-denotation epaulet on one shoulder and a commander's on the other, stepped forward. Triz's gaze ratcheted downward from the officer's epaulets to the sidearm holstered at her left hip. "Captain, I'm going to have to ask you to come with us."

"Of course," Casne said flatly. "I'm happy to assist the Interior Watch any way I can."

"Interior Watch?" Triz's belly lurched, and not from all the drink she'd downed. The Interior Watch served as the Fleet's military police. Like PubWel, but with shocksticks. "Casne, what's going on?"

"Lieutenant," the female officer said, and her junior stepped up with a pair of restraints.

"Hey—no. No!" Triz grabbed the restraints and tossed them over the side of the Arcade. Below, a few surprised voices yelped before the noise of the celebrations swallowed up any dismay. The junior officer took a few steps toward her, then stopped and glanced at his superior. Triz took advantage of the pause to jab a finger into his shoulder.

Inside her own chest, her heart hammered out of kilter like a TR-39 with a misaligned nozzle. "You can't arrest her! Don't you know who she is? What she's done for the Fleet? This is all a misunderstanding, Casne is a common enough name—"

"Triz." Casne's voice was still eerily level, but the ice in it thawed around Triz's name. "I need you to tell my parents where I am in case this isn't all straightened out by the time they wake up tomorrow. I need you to keep a cool head and ask the right questions. Can you do that for me? Triz?"

Triz swallowed hard. Casne's brown eyes, usually so warm and soft, were now diamond drill bits boring into her. Instead of pounding, her heart slowed enough to fit a lifetime between each beat. "I—I can. Shitting stars. Yes, of course."

A crooked smile cracked the hard lines of Casne's face. She bent over to press a kiss between Triz's knitted eyebrows. And then the Watch officer was locking her wrists into the closed cylinders of a second pair of restraints and guiding her forward through a crowd that parted before them. The noisy banter and clatter of bottles receded, falling away into shoes scuffing on the plastic floor and uncomfortable muttering.

Casne would never have done anything to merit this kind of treatment. If she'd ever broken a rule in her life, it was the stupid kind of rule, the ones that needed breaking.

People didn't get hustled up to Justice because they spilled spicewine on the sleeve of their dress uniform. Triz felt very small and entirely useless watching Casne march along that human hallway. She didn't realize she'd dropped the bottle of green wine until it bounced off her toe.

"Nine arms of Swalen, what's going on?" And then

there was Kalo, intercepting the Watch officers before they could hustle Casne out along the Arcade for the rest of the Hab to gawk at. He grabbed the senior officer by the arm hard enough to spin her around. "Is this your idea of a bad joke?"

The Watch officer jerked her arm out of his grasp. "This is none of your concern, *Lieutenant*." Casne stressed his rank as she straightened the black stripes on her shoulder: a hint even Triz could read.

But taking hints had never been Kalo's strong suit. "You're not going anywhere with her." He brandished his wrist fob in the junior officer's direction, making him step back. "I'm calling Commander Escoth. And Admiral Savelian. Whoever I have to get down here to get this straightened out."

"It was Admiral Savelian who issued the order." The junior Watch officer's lips stretched over his teeth: not really a smile, not really a sneer. "Stand down, Lieutenant."

Kalo surveyed the bigger officer for just a moment. Then he hauled back and punched him square in the mouth.

Triz lurched forward with every intention of throwing herself into Kalo's fight. Even if the enemy of her enemy was *also* her enemy, he had the right idea.

"Kalo." Casne's voice cracked out like a lancet gun, killing Triz's resolve.

Triz guiltily dropped her hands.

The officer's arm locked around Kalo's neck, as the flyboy strained to break free, but Casne's voice pulled him up short. Kalo's arms fell limp and the Watch officer let him slide to the floor.

Lanniq stood just behind the officers, shifting his weight from foot to foot. Behind him, Saabe leaned around for a better view. Casne shook her head at them, an almost imperceptible movement.

Saabe skirted the Interior Watch officers to put a tentative hand on Triz's shoulder. She wanted to shrug off the touch, and she wanted it to stay, too. Casne was the one who deserved comfort now. But she stared straight ahead, stone-faced and straight-backed, without catching Triz's eye to offer a wink or head-shake or some kind of shitting reassurance this was going to be all right. Triz's head spun with shock and alcohol alike, but Casne's face was steely and sober.

"Are you at least going to tell us what all this is about?" Kalo asked, still on the floor at the junior officer's feet, one arm wrapped protectively around his belly. Triz didn't think she'd seen a blow come from the junior officer, but her mind was reeling. Her finger bones groaned under the strain of her fists. Kalo spat a thick wad of blood but missed the officer's boot. "I know the Watch likes to keep its secrets. But if the Admiral sent you—"

The Watch commander's chin jutted out. "Check the channels in the morning and read all about it with the rest of the Hab."

So Triz would have to wait to find out alongside Casne's family.

"It's all right." Casne's voice pulled Triz's eyes up to her. The steadiness of her gaze put the gravity back in Triz's world, took all the upside-down and set it back on the ground—albeit in a jumble. She unpeeled her stiff fingers one at a time from her clenched fists. It hurt, but that helped steady Triz too. The Watch officer nudged Casne's shoulder and hustled her forward, but she craned her neck to look back. "Triz. We'll get this figured out."

Triz nodded. She found herself sandwiched between Lanniq's broad shoulders and Saabe's narrower ones while the Watch officers checked Casne's restraints and marched her away into the Arcade. Into the minilift, and up. To Justice. When she disappeared from sight, Triz's breath hitched, and she doubled over. Saabe said, hesitantly, "Do you . . . do you want company for the walk home?"

Saabe's hand froze her arm where Casne's would have warmed it, but she appreciated eir presence anyway. E pulled Triz gently toward the lift. She stopped, unable to believe what had just happened, how they had just left the safety and warmth of Edillo's. She realized Lanniq had left her side. He was standing outside the bar, head bent, listening to another Fleet officer with captain's stripes. Triz didn't recognize the captain's face, but she knew all too well the look of doubt and dismay on Lanniq's. When the captain turned and walked away, Lanniq looked around, then followed. That was odd. Why did they need him specifically, but not Saabe, who served directly alongside Casne? Maybe Triz could track him down later to find out. Maybe he'd even *tell* her, Fleet secrets be damned; he was Casne's friend, too.

As for Kalo, he leaned up against the doorway of the bar —divested of admirers, he kept company with one of Edillo's rags pressed to his nose.

"Thanks," Triz said, and very nearly meant it. But the noise of the Arcade swallowed up the quiet word.

Only Saabe heard, and gave her elbow a reassuring squeeze. "Hey, no problem. How far downhab do you live?" Triz let em lead her to the lifts and tried to focus on the spicewine spinning in her head. Maybe this was all just a lousy bottle-dream.

CHAPTER THREE

SHOULD Triz wake Casne's family? The thought nearly brought up the spicewine still churning in her stomach. She couldn't go tell them what was happening when she had no idea herself. Instead, she spent most of the night lying awake on every flat surface in her rooms: her bed, the hard line of her cheap fold-down sofa, squeezed on the floor next to the toilet. Sleep fled from her. Every time she closed her eyes the image of Casne in a cell flooded her thoughts.

The Watch officers took Casne uphab, to Justice—the same place where the Ceebee leaders brought back from the fight at Golros were stashed. She'd be safe, wouldn't she? Triz thought of Casne sharing a cell with none other than Rocan Melviq, the Unquenchable Scythe, and shivered. No. The Watch was Fleet, and they'd see to it Casne wasn't thrown in with the same people she'd just helped capture. Triz pressed her fingers against the cold plastic of the bathroom floor and tried to make herself believe that.

Long before the full dayshift station lights came on, Triz

made herself stand and pulled a clean worksuit from the drawer under her bed. She stared at her ghastly face in the mirror and dragged her fingers through her snarled hair a few times, but gave up before it could be honestly described as "combed." The lights in her rooms switched off as she shut the door behind her, and her boots sounded too loud in the empty hallway between her place and Casne's parents'.

Her wrist fob opened the door. Casne snuck her the passcode access years ago, back when Triz was still just a stupid teenager sneaking in to fool around with her girlfriend. And to enjoy being in a real quadhome—not that the Tolvian creche a few floors downhab was bad, but . . . a wallport you could watch whatever you wanted on? A food printer that would give you sugarpips if you asked, not just on holidays but *whenever* you asked? It had seemed like heaven to a wide-eyed creche brat.

It *still* seemed pretty nice, compared to Triz's current quarters. Hers were big enough to share with Casne now, or Nantha, or Casne and Nantha, if they both got leave at the same time—but only just. When Triz had been old enough to ask for her own place from PubWel, they'd stationed her just a few rooms down in a pairhome on the same level. Tiny though the pairhome might be, it was still nice to be close to Casne's family, though Triz was glad to have at least a few doors of distance right after Cas upturned the quadhome's life by running off to enlist. Bad enough to drudge alongside Quelian all day in the 'works those next weeks; worse still putting in overtime as a disappointing daughter-substitute at the family dinner table once a week.

Inside the quadhome, the lights were low, in tune with their residents' biorhythms. When Triz settled onto the nest of floor cushions by the wallport, a local light obediently brightened that corner. She preferred to sit in the dark, but it didn't matter. She raised her fob, then hesitated. It would be nice not to have to hear bad news alone. But it would be nicer to hear it and get herself in check before she had to explain everything to Casne's quadparents. She turned on the wallport and slid the volume down.

The first few channels were playing, respectively, a documentary about the construction of Centerpoint Station, an old astronautics display featuring half a dozen retired XL-8 Starslicers and a lot of fireworks, and the latest Astral Noise concert from Croelo Hab.

Triz had just started to convince herself last night's events had all been a bad dream—a dream, somehow, despite having not snatched a single scrap of sleep all night—when her fob finally scanned over to a newschannel.

"—responsible is reported to be Captain Casne Vivik Veling," the newsreader was saying. The footage shook and wobbled: probably shot from a targeting camera in the belly of a Skimmer or some other starfighter. Explosions in red and gold lanced over the wallport screen. The blasts looked too much like the astronautics celebration, except instead of playing out against a background of black, they rippled over the cracked face of an Arcology, one of the little dome habitats that studded the surface of Hedgehome. Tiny dolls spilled from the wound in the plastisteel surface. Not dolls at all, though. Dying planet-siders. Triz's fist ground against her lips as she swallowed hot bile.

The newsreader went on: "Previously hailed as one of the heroes of the battle at Golros, the captain is being held by Fleet Admiralty pending an investigation on charges of war crimes. On the line with us now, we have Mer Dustald-1 Alderly, CFS Vice Admiral, retired, who served with Strategy during the Cluster Campaigns, to discuss what this means for the Fleet. "

"Tactics like these do *not* represent the Fleet I served in." Mer Alderly's voice cracked, with age and with the strain of her agitation. "Maybe it's a little easier to clear a defense installation in record time when you're willing to weaken its base by destroying the friendly civilian habitation downlevel. Those people had suffered enough already at the hands of the Ceebees. The Fleet should have arrived as liberators. Instead this upstart captain made us murderers. And for what? A shot at an early promotion?"

"Vice Admiral, do you believe that when the charges are read tomorrow, we'll learn wh—"

Triz slammed her wrist fob against the wallport and the screen went black and silent. She rested her forehead against the wallport for the space of a long, shuddering breath, and when she sat back, another light had gone on in the quadhome.

Quelian stood in the space between the portlounge and the galley. Already dressed for the workday, in a gray worksuit nearly the twin of Casne's uniform, the rich undertones of his skin, the copper and bronze of exposed wires, had bled away; he looked like his own ghost. He'd always been a small man, practically a miniature next to his statuesque spouses and daughter, but now he'd all but shriveled away. "We ate with her last night," he said. "She didn't say anything about this."

"It's not true." Triz's fists balled in the soft fabric of her trousers. "Casne would never—she'd *never*. Someone's doing this to, I don't know, get back at her for Golros. Or something!"

Quelian shook his head. "Fleet service changes people.

When you fire a Tactics array long enough, you start to forget what you're firing at. *Who* you're firing at." His lips thinned and he looked away from Triz. "This quad builds and the Fleet destroys. We'll be lucky if the whole family isn't dragged down with that kind of reputation tagged to our name."

"Your reputation?" Triz flung a pillow at him, but he raised a hand, and it bounced harmlessly to the floor. "That's your daughter you're talking about!"

Casne's mother, Veling, peered out of the bedroom doorframe. Idha and Othine, Casne's daddy and damu, were just behind her. "What's going on?" she asked. "What's this about Casne?"

Quelian stared at the ceiling just over his wife's head. The vein in his forehead quivered as his jaw clenched. "Your daughter's been arrested," he said through his teeth. "War crimes, they're saying, and by what I just saw, they're not wrong."

Othine gasped. Idha, forehead furrowed, put his hand on eir shoulder. They both looked to Veling to speak first, which was exactly what she did. "That's absurd." Veling resembled her daughter so strongly; the sudden tears tracing the lines of her face carved a fresh canyon of grief through Triz. "That's Casne you're talking about. No child of this quad would do such a thing, Quelian, you should be ashamed of yourself for even thinking—"

"I came here to see what we were going to do about it." Triz pushed to a stand and stumbled on the uneven footing of the shifting cushions. "I didn't think you were going to . . . Quelian, you're a Justice tribune. Can't you talk to the Fleet? To Admiral Savelian or the—the Interior Watch?"

"He can't pull strings for her now." Veling's word rasped

sandpaper-rough over Triz's skin. "Even if those strings were attached to something worth unraveling, and Triz, I don't know that they are. The Admiralty doesn't, and shouldn't, come running when a tribune snaps their fingers. You know that. How would it look if her father tried to use his influence like that?"

"I know." The words broke out of Triz, a surrender she wasn't ready to signal. "Do you—?" The question died unasked in her mouth, and she swallowed it, fetid and whole.

Unasked, but not unanswered. "No. I don't believe Casne could ever do such a thing." Her eyes cut sideways at Quelian. "Of course, people change. But what you're talking about is more than just *change*. My daughter didn't suddenly abdicate her entire sense of self after five years in the Fleet."

". . . Okay." Triz's hands had balled into fists in the fabric of her worksuit. She pressed her fingers flat instead, smoothing over the deep lines she'd creased in. "I just want to do something. I need to do something. What do I *do*?"

"Go to work," Quelian said. "There's a pile of Skimmers waiting for us in the wrenchworks and a Parallax moored outside that's not going to spontaneously regenerate its lateral atmospheric stabilizer."

"Quelian." Veling's voice lanced into her quadspouse like a well-cracked whip. Quelian flinched and looked away. "You will *not* take this out on Triz." Veling pushed past him to take Triz's hands in her own and cast a frown over her shoulder, which Quelian ignored. Veling and Quelian had always been the most diagonal in this quad, both doting on their single quadborn child in their own ways. Veling had always been especially kind to the guttergirl stray who had fallen into the family's orbit.

"We're going to figure this out," Othine said, putting on

a smile—for Triz's sake, she thought. "The people of Vivik know you and trust your judgment. And they know and trust Casne, too."

Veling nodded, squeezing Triz's fingers. Her strong hands ground Triz's finger-bones together but Triz welcomed the pressure. "Hells if you're picking up a wrench today, my heart. Quelian can work himself senseless down there if he needs to, but you don't have to."

Triz squeezed Veling's hands back, if not as hard. She didn't know whether she wanted the mindless release of work or not, but she did know she wanted more than just that. "I need to do something," she repeated softly.

"They'll let us visit her, if she's in holding in the Hab." Veling released her grip and straightened the silk wrap that smoothed her hair for the night. A tear dripped off the tip of her chin, and she ignored it. "We can take shifts, keep her company, bring her—I don't know. Bring her whatever she needs."

"Nantha." That single word sucked the air out of the room faster than a hull breach. Triz struggled for the air to say it again. Guilt filled her lungs instead. Why hadn't she thought of that sooner? Visions exploded in front of her: a stone-faced Fleet clerical worker breaking the news through a brief port connection, or worse yet, a terse text missive delivered straight to Nantha's fob. "I'll call her," Triz said. "Tell her what's happening."

"Thank you." Veling folded her arms. With her chin lifted high, she looked more like Casne than ever. The space in the room shifted, Othine and Idha drawing closer together, standing behind Veling. Their positions made Quelian's lone outpost by the far wall all the more conspicuous. "Now, we have some quad business to discuss amongst ourselves before Quelian goes anywhere. If you'll excuse us, Triz."

* * *

NANTHA ANSWERED the call after the first ring. On the wallport in the wrenchworks, her face was porcelain-pale with dark smears under the eyes. "Triz?" Nantha asked, "Do you have any news?"

Triz stared up at Nantha's bigger-than-life features on the oversized wallport surrounded by tools and parts hung on the walls. Veling told her not to go to work today, but a retreat to her own empty rooms was unthinkable. At least here the hulks of sleeping starfighters kept her company, and the dull throb of vacuums and cleaner modules filled the silence.

"Hi, Nantha," Triz said. "Someone . . . already told you." If only she could wish away the millions of miles between them and wrap Nantha up in her arms. If only she'd been the one to call Nan first—she shied away from that guilty thought. "Are you all right?"

"Not particularly." Nantha looked away. Her dark hair was mussed, and so was her usually pristine uniform. By Fleet Standard Time, it was midmorning on Hask, the substation just outside Centerpoint where Nantha was billeted, but Triz suspected she'd woken Nan up. "I don't think I'll be all right until this all gets straightened out. Or I at least get to talk to her." Nan folded over at the waist. Triz's stomach churned as she watched Nan's fingers twist through her close-cropped hair. When she spoke again, her voice was muffled by her knees. "They have footage, Triz! How can it be real?"

"I don't know," Triz said. She felt so useless. "I don't know anything. I'm so sorry, Nan." Triz gnawed the inside of her cheek. In the cozy picture she carried in her mind, Nantha was always laughing, always in the middle of some dreadful but cheery punchline. She found it hard to reconcile the woman in front of her with that image. But it wasn't as hard as reconciling her conception of Casne with the woman hauled away in restraints the night before. "Did they call you last night after they brought her in?"

Nantha pushed out of her forward fold into a boneless slouch. "Kalo called," Nan answered, her teeth digging into her chapped lower lip. "He wanted me to hear it from him before I got the Fleet's official notice. Or saw it on the port. Have you been watching?"

"I've been trying not to. You shouldn't, either." Better not to pour pollution into her remaining reserves of strength. "They'll tell us what we need to know." Triz didn't even know who *they* were. The Fleet? Justice?

"I hope so, because she didn't. Even if it was an accident, a miscalculated firing sequence—why didn't she just *tell* us?" Nantha's voice broke and the edges were sharp. "Did she tell you?"

"No!" Triz pressed her hand to the wallport. It was faintly warm to the touch, and after a moment, Nantha mirrored the gesture. "Nan, did they take you off active duty?"

A rough laugh. "Of course. I can't be plugged into Nav calculations right now. I'd probably accidentally point half the Fleet into the Cluster and chart a few courses straight through the heart of a neutron star." Her voice steadied. "I know she couldn't have told you anything, because there's nothing to tell. I know Casne. It's just all happening so fast and so far away—"

"I know." Triz let her hand fall back into her lap. Nantha's hand stayed on the port screen, a ghostly white afterimage left behind by Triz's fingers. "I feel like I'm in shock, and I'm right here." And whatever else might be between them, Triz wasn't Casne's wife. "I can't imagine what it's like, Nantha."

"You *are* there, though." Nantha's fingers spasmed and she leaned closer to the wallport. "Be my eyes and ears. Keep an eye on her. And Triz, if you can get to the bottom of this—!" Her hand dropped away and she bent over her wrist fob. "I'm shooting you the names of some of the officers on the Dailos. People Casne knows, who know her. Maybe one of them can help you work through this."

That sounded more like the Nantha Triz knew, but the sudden steel in her made Triz wilt. "If anyone's going to get this straightened out, it's whoever Justice assigns her as an Advocate. Not me. I'm just a wrenchworks jockey."

"Advocates are Fleet officers." Nantha's blue eyes snapped down to the wallport inputs, then back up to Triz. "Can you promise me it's not someone in the Fleet pinning this on Casne for some reason?"

"No, but . . . " Triz hadn't considered that possibility, and she didn't like considering it now. But the Fleet was made up of people, and people could do ugly things. Turn an uncaring eye to the gutterkids scurrying beneath the decks of Rydoine Hab, for example. Or slice through their own flesh to turn themselves into Ceebees. "I'll help however I can, Nan, but—"

"I know you will." Nantha half-smiled and Triz's doubt

sublimated into ever-expanding resolve. "Go see her first. She'll need a friendly face. Even more than I did."

"Her parents were going to see her . . . " Triz hesitated. *Some* of her parents were, at least.

Nantha read into that silence. "She'll need all the strength they can lend her and all of yours too. Give her my love, Triz. Please."

"I will."

"And take care of yourself. You know we love you." Nan managed an echo of a smile. Her hand finally fell away from the wallport screen as its light flickered out. Around her, the low hum of the machinery was a distant comfort. The ships, ringed around the airlock at the 'works center, stood on their pedestals like statues of old friends. Triz put one hand on the ventral hatch of a DX-3 Nebula and leaned into it, taking strength from its vast weight. When her arm dropped back to her side, she was ready to lose herself in the monotony of work again.

WHEN QUELIAN ARRIVED in the wrenchworks, late in the morning, Triz was up to her shoulders in a Swarmer's innards. She knew her way around a ship, at least, and she couldn't make the damage any worse—which was a lot more than she could say about trying to solve Casne's case. What did a stupid guttergirl know about the inner workings of Justice, or the Fleet? "Glad to see you're keeping yourself together," Quelian said, pressing his lips together.

Triz realized, with a flinch, that he was . . . proud of her? "Sure," she said, not trusting her voice to go uncracked on more than one syllable.

"I've got some screenwork to catch up on before I join you out here." There was a closed-down look to him today. There was always a closed-down look to Quelian, really, but now it was as if he'd added a rotary combination and a maglock into the mix. "I'll be in the offices for now."

Triz flashed him a sounds-good gesture and focused back on the ship in front of her. When the office door banged shut behind her, she let out a planetquake of a breath. While the repair job she was currently working on did require her to rip open this panel and get intimate with the ship's computer systems, it did not require her to try to download those systems' logs to her personal datablocks.

This was the third Swarmer she'd tried—surely one of them had captured vid that would prove Casne innocent—but every single one had been doubly locked down beneath Fleet access codes and Justice inquest screeners. Triz considered asking Lanniq or Saabe to log in under their own officer-level access codes (a wrenchworks account only got you so far, and she wasn't exactly running diagnostics here). But you had to rank somewhere just shy of the Seventh God of Issam to merit access to this data. Triz wasn't on speaking terms with any of the admiralty and/or Godhead.

What was she even doing here? She knew functionally nothing at all about Justice or Fleet actions or, really, anything beyond getting the engine of XR-2 to stop knocking under maximum thrust. Stupid to think she could do something useful. In the end, she was really just a hopped-up guttergirl with a little good socialization.

She could hear Casne's weary retort to that. *If you call yourself stupid again, Triz . . .*

Fine. Not stupid, then. But very, very frustrated. Triz fobbed into the magistrate's scheduling system to check on the appointment she'd requested with Casne. It had been bumped an hour later in the afternoon, but still lit up green—request accepted.

Another hour to kill.

Triz headed to the next workbay over and crawled underneath the imbalanced rear engine suite of a Gyrax 33. She finished repairs on the Gyrax, and one of the Skimmers that was only a cracked plastiglass panel the worse for the wear. Quelian would take them out for a spin later to make sure they were spaceworthy before handing them back to their usual pilots.

Triz hadn't been out in the black since the trip over from Rydoine and didn't plan on another such jaunt anytime soon.

Or *any* time.

The work absorbed her, filled her mind with joint seals and line reroutes. Triz felt like a different person when she worked, and sometimes she thought she liked this person better than the one she saw in the mirror every morning and night.

A few minutes before her scheduled slot uphab, Triz went to wash up in the wrenchworks sink. But as she splashed water on her stained hands, her wrist fob chirped. Her appointment had been bumped back another two hours. She gnawed her lip and went to find something left-over to eat in the 'works coldcase. She indulged in a pair of dumplings from a tin marked with the name QUELIAN in bold hand on the lid—it had been there four days now, and if he wasn't going to eat Casne's daddy's cooking, then he couldn't complain if Triz cut his losses—then she started the necessary disassembly of Kalo's fighter. When she hit a good stopping place, she stashed her tools.

Quelian still hadn't emerged from the office. That could be either good or bad. He didn't like screenwork for screenwork's sake, but if he had moved on from invoices and supply ordering to using the resources of Justice to help Casne out . . .

Wishful thinking. Triz washed up and hit the lift. Two floors up and her fob chirped again.

Another delay. Another four hours.

The lift wall kissed Triz's forehead coldly where she rested it. Going back down to the wrenchworks now would be a retreat. Casne would never retreat—well, no, that was stupid, with Casne's head for strategy she'd definitely retreat if she had to. But if Nantha were in trouble, or even Triz?

No way.

Triz queried the quadparents' fobs too for schedule updates: only Veling had time marked off for an official visit time with Casne, and while Triz was looking, that too leaped half a day into the future. This time, Triz ordered her fob not to reschedule. Standing up, she crossed her arms and tried to look like someone who could stroll into Justice and demand access to one of its prisoners.

The stern set of her face didn't last for long. Triz scanned her fob at the entrance to Justice and ducked through the open door. She froze. The queues in front of the long semicircular counter were jam-packed with petitioners who needed fines disputed, fobs registered and recycled, and any other manner of bureaucratic nonsense. All the color of the Arcade just below Triz's feet bled away up here, leaving nothing but clean, functional lines and serious gray and beige. But the noise was still the same.

One of the lane operators popped out at her: Belas Vivik Fithe, a Justice clerk who lived down the hall from Casne's quadhome. Triz queued up in the line under his number and tried not to fidget like a child with her jacket or her fob.

Belas greeted her warmly despite the circumstances and nodded when Triz showed him the two appointment delays on her fob. When she asked if she could see Casne anyway, as long as she was uphab, he squinted at the screen of his deskport.

"You know I shouldn't do that." He glanced at the clerks on either side of him and leaned in. "I shouldn't tell you the Fleet is trying to isolate her while they press her to confess. Fleet hero, ugly business. They don't want a messy, noisy trial to detract from parading around all the Cyberbionautics brass they've brought in." He fiddled with his fob, and his lane number flickered in the air, then vanished. The queue behind Triz groaned. "I also shouldn't ask you to come with me while I go on my break." Belas stood. "So. I won't ask. Follow me."

Triz met him at a gap in the long, semicircular counter. He ushered her to the central ring room at the top of the Hab, where Justice made its home. The only thing farther uphab was the room where Justice held hearings, and she would just as soon not think about that place right now. "I happen to know Fleet Counsel is taking their lunch," he murmured. "I'll pop you in to see Casne for a few minutes."

Triz followed. She wanted to embrace the plan wholeheartedly, but she knew Justice kept eyes on the whole station, and on *itself* most of all. Concern overwrote desire, and she grabbed Belas' sleeve. "But won't you get in trouble? Belas, I don't want you to lose your job."

He stopped so hard Triz ran into his side. "My niece is studying the alien intelligences on Golros. She and her outpost were there when the Ceebees launched their terraformers. If the Fleet hadn't gotten there when they did, well . . . " He waved one hand beside his head. "Makes my skin crawl having them locked up here till Quelian's replacement can get here." Triz didn't know what that meant, but Belas was still talking. "If Justice started in with the hearings this morning like they'd planned, I might've been clear of the lot by eighteen-hundred hours. It's not as if there's a lot of *uncertainty* at play. Rocan has shown who he is in more ways than I'd care to count."

He leaned in conspiratorially. "Now, I know their implants are disabled, but I don't trust that lot as far as I can throw them under five G's. The Ceebees have plans within plans. Even when they're sleeping, they're cooking up new ways to get what they want." He gently tugged her hand free of his coat. "Well! Never you mind all that. As far as my job goes? Oh, silly Belas, didn't check the schedule for permissions when a heartbroken wife came a-crying to him."

Triz felt a flush of red heat color her cheeks. "Oh—we're not married."

Belas shrugged and smiled gently. "Silly Belas." He reached to fob a door into another, smaller ring, but it opened first.

The person who hurried through, head down, was Lanniq, ashen-faced and mouth-pinched. Were Fleet friends not getting their visits turned aside the way civilians were? Or had he been called in for his testimony?

"Lanniq," Triz called, and he jumped. She wanted to ask him what he knew about Casne's case but found herself blurting instead: "Are you all right?"

"Sorry, Triz. Can't talk right now." He gave her a tight-lipped smile, not meeting her eyes, and kept walking. He was definitely *not* okay. Triz swallowed a polite goodbye. An even worse theory popped into Triz's head: maybe Lanniq was one of the ones urging Casne to confess. She watched him go until Belas tugged her forward and into the centermost part of Justice.

The cells of Justice formed the inside ring of the Hab level, each cell a pie slice that narrowed nearly to a point in the middle. Belas dropped a chair in front of one cell, which made its occupant sit up on her cot. Triz tried not to look too hard at the other cells, but found herself staring anyway. In them, people sat or slept with missing eyes or limbs, with transparent gel wraps clinging to the empty space where a section of skull or skin should have been. The Ceebee prisoners were deprived of certain enhancements, the ones with offensive capabilities, as Belas had said. Justice fried their nanobots with a fixative pulse when they were captured.

"I'll be down at the wallport if you need me," Belas said, and Triz jerked her attention back to him. "Hurry. I don't know how soon Counsel will get back."

"Thank you." Triz tried to put all her gratitude into those words, but they broke apart under the weight. She slid into the chair he left for her and looked up into Casne's face. Only the barrier of the cell lay between them; it shimmered in the same shade of dismal gray as the floor, the cots, the walls; even, it seemed, the wan lighting. Weary lines carved their way between Casne's brows and around the corners of her mouth. Triz wanted to reach through the barrier and smooth them out, to reshape Casne's mask of exhaustion into one of quiet, tranquil slumber.

Triz swallowed hard. "Hi, Cas."

"They told me I wasn't allowed to see anyone." Casne's voice came out thick as day-old algae starter. But that wasn't true, was it? Hadn't Lanniq just been here? Who else would he have needed to speak to but Casne? But before Triz could press her on that, Casne went on the offensive. "What did you *do* to get in here, Triz?"

"Nothing!" Triz changed the subject before Casne could worm the lie out of her. "I wanted to see if you needed anything, or if you—if there was anything I could do."

"I'm all right." An instinctual response. Casne's mouth tightened. "They won't let me talk to Nantha, either."

"I just spoke with her a little while ago. She's all right." A look of bleak understanding passed between them. "Your quad sends their love too." That, at least, bought an unqualified smile from Casne. Too bad it wasn't the unqualified truth. "Casne, what's going on? Nothing I saw on the port makes any sense."

The gates of Casne's face slammed shut. Her expression might as well have been cut from steel for all the give in it. That wasn't the Casne Triz knew, but that fit the pattern of the past day. "I don't think I'm allowed to talk to you about that, Triz, not with an ongoing investigation. I don't know what's happening, but I know what I did at Golros and I stand by it. And that's all I can say to you, really."

"Sure. Fleet business. I understand." Triz didn't understand at all. "How long until your . . . trial?" Just saying the word out loud hurt.

"I have to face trifold Justice," said Casne, a little tiredly. "A Fleet tribune, another from the Watch, and someone the civilian court at Centerpoint will send. They'll take a week to get here, or so I'm told."

"A civilian tribune?" Triz shook her head but didn't manage to shake off her confusion. "Why wait? We have six of those here on Vivik."

Casne's shoulders dropped a few centimeters. "Only

one with enough experience markers to hear a war crimes trial. And he had to recuse himself for reasons of partiality."

"Oh. *Oh.*" Of course Quelian couldn't hear Casne's case. Triz's arms wrapped around herself. It was good Quelian was required to recuse himself; less good that any concerns of partiality might not go the way Casne thought. Casne had been far away for most of the anger her departure had provoked, and Triz had never been entirely sure how much of Quelian's disappointment bled through port calls and family messages. She'd be damned if Casne had to weather Quelian's disdain now, with all the rest of the meteor shower currently pelting her. "Is there anything I can bring you? Or do?"

"Prove the evidence was faked, figure out who did it." A humorless smile pinched Casne's lips. "Maybe get me a promotion for my troubles?"

"Oh, is that all." Triz's throat dried up, and she forced a smile. Fleet rules be damned, Casne put her confidence and her trust in Triz. "Failing that, I could try to smuggle you in some of your damu's biscuits. Belas likes me—by which I mean, he likes you. I bet he'd let me."

"Just ask around. There were dozens of Swarmers attached to the Dailos alone, array techs on the other whales. Everyone's got eyes."

"Give me something to go on," Triz begged. "Who you think is behind it! Or why it's happening."

"I can't, Triz. Really. I already said that."

Triz's hands twisted in her lap. "You can't tell *me* anything. But did you tell Lanniq while *he* was here?"

Casne's stone-smooth expression creased into a frown. "What? When?"

"Ah! If it isn't the Hero of Golros," a new, sickly voice said.

Triz jumped. Casne looked past Triz's shoulder and her eyes narrowed.

The man they both feared was being marched down the corridor between two guards. Triz felt her shoulders tense into iron knots. Rocan.

He felt for his cot, then took a seat and smiled at Triz, who blanched at the sight of him. She knew that face, even with both eyes replaced by hollow sockets. He'd ported a video when he put out his own eyes and replaced them with optimized electronic replacements. Unlike most of the rest of her creche class, Triz had never watched it and never wanted to. "Perhaps when they forge the medal of honor, they'll weld a pair of restraints on directly, just to save some time and effort."

Triz's mouth worked soundlessly a few times. She managed to sputter: "What is—what is *he* doing here?" Of all the people Casne could be imprisoned with, why did it have to be Rocan Dustald-3 Melviq, the very man whose movement Casne and the Fleet had worked to annihilate over the past months? No one had more of a reason to punish Casne—and now, no one had a better chance of access to her. Triz's hands flexed at her sides. "You shouldn't be locked up in here with monsters like him. They couldn't hold you on one of the whaleships instead?"

"Indeed! It's frankly barbaric that a visiting head of state should have to suffer the company of a known war criminal." The holes in Rocan's face held Triz's attention; even deprived of his implants, he seemed to be staring at her, boring holes through her to match his own. "Apparently, our settlement of clusterward space has been ill-received in the Confederated Worlds."

The guards guided Rocan into a cell and sealed the barrier behind him. "Citizen," said the senior officer, turning to Triz. "Casne Vivik Veling isn't authorized for visitors at this time."

"You destroyed two Habs and an Arcology to take Hedgehome!" Triz ignored the guard. Her lip curled in disdain. "You almost exterminated the native intelligence on Golros."

"I think you'll find we have recorded evidence to show that it was our friend the Captain here who demolished the Arcology on Hedgehome." Rocan counted on his fingers. "And the Habs were given instructions to evacuate; their choices to the contrary don't rest on my shoulders. That sets us at a tie, although I'm disinclined to measure Golros' so-called alien . . . 'intelligence' against the actual *human* lives ended by Captain Casne. And what more do you suppose the Interior Watch will turn up if they start going through footage of the previous combat she's seen?"

"Citizen—" The guard put his hand on Triz's shoulder.

She shrugged it off, jumping away from him. He didn't want to hurt her or overpower her, and she used his reluctance against him, dancing around a chair in the corridor to buy herself another moment. "You can't leave her in here with him!"

"I didn't kill those people." Casne spoke to Rocan as if no one else were in the room. Her lips pressed bloodlessly together as she remembered the rules that compelled her not to talk about her case. She jerked her head side to side. "And your math doesn't check out."

"Casne is a hero," Triz spat, putting herself between the two cells, "and you're the human in a robot suit who thought he could get away with stealing two planets out from under the rest of the galaxy. Don't you dare compare yourself to her."

Rocan smiled. Unlike the wreckage of his eyes, his teeth were all too human, neatly lined up but faintly yellow for their years. "She's more like me than she is like you, a grease stain someone forgot to wipe off the floor of the wrenchworks."

This time the guard's hands closed around both of Triz's arms. "Say your goodbyes, citizen. It's time to go."

"Is that a Rydoine accent I detect in you as well?" Rocan pressed. "But not an upper Hab accent, I think. Was it the good captain who pulled you out of the recycling pits and raised you up to something like humanity? Or have you just attached yourself to her for the duration, like a watersys barnacle with delusions of grandeur?"

"Shut up," Triz said in disgust. The same words cracked out of Casne with a force Triz couldn't have matched on her best day. The pure acid of Casne's tone surprised Triz. It occurred to her that she didn't really know who Casne was, couldn't swear that the woman who flew for the Fleet and the one who sat down at Remembrance dinners in the quad-home were one and the same. Sometimes it hurt to remember that distance, but right now, she reflected Casne's incandescent anger like a tiny, angry moon. She didn't believe, not for a second, that either of those women could've destroyed a living Hab. "Shut. Up."

"I think we're done here." The guards steered Triz away from the cells, gently but firmly. She craned her neck, wanting one last image of her to leave with.

"It's okay, Triz," Casne called after her. Triz planted her

feet, pulling the guards up short. "The Fleet will do the right thing by me." Casne might even believe that. Triz, on the other hand . . . "Just . . . look after my folks. This must be awful for them." She leaned toward Triz, her forehead glimmering faintly where it touched the barrier. "And for you. This was supposed to be a happy visit."

"So we'll have twice as much celebrating to do, once you're out." Triz put her full effort into a grin that quickly ran out of fuel. "Cas . . . if they do figure this out and let you off, is your career going to be okay?"

"The Fleet will do the right thing by me," Casne repeated, which was not at all the same as "yes."

When the door closed behind Triz and the guards, it felt like closing the recycling pit hatch on a burial.

CHAPTER FOUR

TRIZ DRIFTED DOWNWARD FROM JUSTICE, first across the open escalators down to the Arcade, and then around each spiraling level, past the 'shine sellers with their sputtering still and the sizzling griddles of fatty sausages and flatbreads, past strings of beads and squares of shimmering scalecloth. Usually, any spare time to browse the Arcade would be a welcome holiday, but right now, every step raised her blood pressure. Unbelievable, that everyone else went on with their lives while Casne was pinned in Justice above.

And yet when she reached the lowest level of the Arcade, Triz gravitated to a lift and fobbed in a request to be carried downhab. The wrenchworks exerted as much pull on her as the local star did to the Hab. The wrenchworks was a place where she always knew which end was up. *Everything* was up when you hung out at the bottom of the Hab all the time.

But when the lift doors opened, Triz found she wasn't alone. Quelian had stripped the warped plastiglass from the cockpit of a Skimmer. The plastiglass reformed its original shape after an impact or even a puncture, but when over-heated by the superheated blast of a plasma cannon, the substructure memory of its original architecture was destroyed. He'd begun to paint a layer of sealant on the cockpit frame to prepare it for the replacement.

The soft swish of the lift doors closing behind Triz made him look up and push his goggles to his forehead. "Good, you're here. Losing the morning's got us behind schedule, and the bursar will want a discount for every day, every *minute* we delay in getting these things back to them."

Triz walked to the wallmount, picked up a wrench, and turned it back and forth in her hand. She was tempted to take the wrench to the discarded piece of plastiglass, but of course, the whole point of plastiglass was that it wouldn't break except under a level of stress much greater than an angry mechanic could produce. "Is that what you're worried about?" she asked. "Having to offer the Fleet a discount?"

Quelian set the sealant hose aside and leaned on the nose of the Skimmer with both hands. His face showed no emotion, but a telltale flush of his forehead betrayed him. "What should I be doing? Tearing my clothes, screaming and wailing? Should I smear my face with mourning paint and say my prayers over the recycler hatch?"

"She's not dead." Triz replaced the wrench and chose a bolt extractor instead, which she carried over to Kalo's fighter. She remembered the conversation with Nan and the thought of Kalo calling her like he was practically a part of their family still burned her. The cold core at the heart of that fire whispered: *Maybe they'd rather have him in their gon than me.* No—she shrugged off that selfish thought. At least *someone* had remembered Nan.

But she'd rather get Kalo's Skimmer back in fighting trim

and have him out of her hair sooner than later, especially if the alternative was him haunting her for the next week. The respiration cells on the shitting thing weren't letting air flow through; Triz hated greenwork but even starfighter pilots needed to breathe. She climbed atop the Swarmer, just behind the cockpit, and began to work the paneling above the cells loose. "She's in Justice. Stop acting like they're the same."

"I'd ask you to stop acting like you can see stars between the two." Quelian pounded on the Skimmer's wing. The impact sent the sealant hose skittering away; it crashed to the ground beneath the fighter and he barked a curse. He dropped down heavily beside the fallen hose. "I know how you feel about each other." The absence of the word *love* there sent supernova sparks up behind Triz's eyes. "But she's not the same woman who left Vivik, and that's something we all have to come to terms with."

Triz wrenched the paneling free, and a barked laugh came along with it. Now here was something she could do for Casne: throw herself on the grenade of Quelian's anger. "That's what this is all still about? She was never going to take over the wrenchworks. She never had the sense for a busted ship, let alone the ins and outs of every make and model that comes through here." It felt good to say the things to Quelian that she'd balanced on the tip of her tongue for years. Maybe a little too good. Was her anger for Casne's benefit or her own? She frowned and started working the algae cells free from their frame. "Isn't that why you keep me around? Because you needed a spare?"

"Don't turn this around on me." Quelian threw the hose back up over the top of the fighter but didn't follow it up.

"My daughter made her decisions. You not liking how they came out doesn't erase them."

Triz's tongue worked its way out between her teeth as she ripped off panels; now she bit it hard. "And you not liking them doesn't make a war crime out of a rough goodbye!" Each algae cell she pulled free was brown, and their gelatinous enclosures were hardened from their usually soft state. Too dry? She flipped the frame over to check the intake and found it crusted over reddish-brown. Flakes fell away when her fingertips brushed against the ragged coating; she let the cell frame fall back against the Skimmer as she crawled forward and into the open cockpit.

Her work gloves dropped into her lap as her bare fingers searched the smooth, cold interior of the plastiglass cockpit shell. Ah: there it was. Someone untrained in the arts of the wrenchworks might not have been able to find it, but yes, a small, irregular dimple marked the place where the plastiglass had slowly closed back around a puncture. Some piece of microdebris or shrapnel had penetrated the cockpit. She turned to kneel against the pilot's seat; someone had scrubbed this side of the air return intake clean, but she could see more ragged crust peeking through from the other side. Her heart hammered in her ears. The knot of frustration tying up her guts over the past months unraveled: not in relief, but in a wild expansion that balled up in her fists and closed off her throat.

The algae cells had died because the air intake was blocked by dried blood.

"Triz!" The banging of her heart echoed back from the wrenchworks. She blinked. Quelian was pounding the hose nozzle against the Skimmer's fuselage. He stopped only when she fixed him with a hollow stare. "Have you heard a single word I've said?"

"I've heard plenty." She unwound herself from the cockpit and slid over the side of the fighter to the floor. She didn't land as neatly as Quelian, catching herself with one hand on the fuselage before she could fall. "I'm sorry I'm not her. If that's what you're wishing. If I were the one locked up in a Justice cell, she'd be doing everything she could to get me out. She wouldn't hole up here in the works wishing things were different. So I guess I'm going to do what she would." Turning her back on Kalo's Skimmer and on Quelian too, she let herself stride back toward the lift.

"Don't you walk away from this wrenchworks!" Quelian shouted. "Veling is a recycling engineer, not the shitting owner of this place. *I* am, and she doesn't get to give you a bereavement day to roll around moaning."

"Then I quit." Triz mashed the lift call button with her knuckles and kept her back to Quelian as she waited. Better not to see his face just now. Maybe the other quadparents would try to walk her words back later; maybe they wouldn't be able to. At this moment Triz didn't really care one way or another. "I'll be back for my stuff later. Right now, I'm going to go save your daughter."

Anger or shock leached the strength from Quelian's words. They ripped ragged out of him and fluttered helplessly, begging for Triz's attention. "If you walk out of here now, you won't get the wrenchworks when I kick on. I've got more than enough time to train up another wrench and if you don't think there's a dozen pups on this Hab who would jump at the chance—"

"Then I'll take my luck waiting around to see who PubWel and the Distribution Council choose to hand the works over to." Triz shrugged, a tight little jerk of the shoulders that cranked up her tension rather than releasing it. "If not, I'll hitch a ride to some other Hab." The thought of launching herself out there—out into that bottomless darkness—of long empty days unmoored from any Hab, sent a tremor down her spine.

"I like my odds," she finished.

Something heavy crashed behind her, metal yelping against metal. "Over my dead body!"

"Maybe." Triz tried to shrug and failed. "Or maybe the Council will redistribute early if I give them a reason to think the wrenchworks would do better under new ownership." Finally, the lift doors opened. Triz turned as she entered.

Quelian's eyes watered in his flushed face; she'd really pissed him off this time. Triz drank that down and found it tasted good, despite the skim of guilt floating on top.

"Remember," Triz said. "You're the one who walked away first. Not from the wrenchworks. From everything that really matters."

The doors closed between them, and Triz waited until she was two levels up before she slammed both fists against the hard metal of the lift door.

CHAPTER FIVE

THAT NIGHT TRIZ used her fob to pull up a list to her tiny port screen: officers who'd served with, under, or near Casne aboard the Dailos. A few names she knew, most she didn't. She prowled the edges of the Arcade, looking for the precise shade of gray fatigues that distinguished a Fleetie from any other random Hab resident. The first woman whose sweaty sleeve she caught outside the heliodrome track turned her away with only a few terse words. "Fleet business. Anything you're entitled to know, you can find out in Justice." Triz had a few terse words for her, too: the kind that had two other Fleet officers closing ranks on either side.

The next officer Triz managed to flag down had just emerged from an hour in the Cosset. Triz wasn't used to visiting the row of pleasure-houses on the Arcade; she tried not to stare past him into the Cosset for a better look. When he stepped to the side of the busy main Arcade footwalk to speak with her, the flowery smells of tea and honey wine clung to him, as did the stronger, more intense scent of sex.

The wine made him more pliable to her questioning than the last officer, and he didn't seem to notice when Triz breathed unsubtly through her mouth.

"I mean, I didn't see anything. I remember the Arcology blowing, but that's hard to miss unless you're already in a tailspin. When you're behind the yoke, it's best to keep an eye on what's right ahead of you. And behind. What the whales were up to, no idea. Maybe one of the other pilots got a better peek." He hesitated. "It doesn't sound like the captain? But I'm not a Tactics geek, so I don't know how well I can talk about it."

Triz thanked him for his time and let him stagger off to other more relaxing pursuits.

She paused for a moment outside the massive window at the edge of the Arcade to watch a small squadron of Swarmers—four Skimmers flanking an oversized Arcwing—running drills just outside the Hab. Hard to imagine what it was like being out there in the darkness all the time. She didn't even like the rare type of wrenchwork that took her outside the Hab in a vac suit to walk the wounded skin of a cargo freighter or passenger transport. Her mouth puckered with the bitter tang of resentment: not that she'd be doing any of that kind of thing any time soon, or possibly ever again.

The closest Skimmer feinted sharply toward the Hab and made her flinch and jump back from the window. What was that pilot doing? But the Skimmer stopped short of the plas-tiglass and she felt the gentle *tink* of a light touch against the Hab wall. Such a tiny sound; an unpleasant reminder of just how fragile Light Attack Swarmers really were.

"Hey, don't worry, Lanniq's just running drills," a voice said, startling her. It was Saabe. E'd found her before she could press off in search of another Fleet uniform to grill. "Emergency Hab penetration, that kind of thing. Don't worry, during drills they don't plant real charges so this part of the Arcade shouldn't be sucking vacuum momentarily." Eir grin of greeting faded. "I hear you've been on the prowl for information."

Triz glared at em but tagged along at eir elbow as e started walking along the Arcade's outer path. "You think Justice and the Watch care more about getting this investigation right than I do? Especially when that's my—" The words *wife* or *gonmate* jammed in her throat on sharp, false edges. "When it's Casne involved? They've got a million high-ranking Ceebees to put on trial. They'll broadcast those trials across the Confederated Worlds, and I'm supposed to be sure they're doing their due diligence on *one* interior hearing? Especially one they'd prefer didn't make a big quake through the newschannels?"

Saabe sighed. "I'm not arguing with you. Admiralty's had their eye on Casne for a while now—not like that," e hastily explained at Triz's scowl. "Commendations, fast promotions. I'm afraid they'll come down hard on her. Make it clear they don't play favorites."

Triz didn't like the sound of that. "Do you have any idea who could be behind this, though? Or how? Any way the Ceebees could've reprogrammed a firing pattern? Taken control of the firing array without Cas noticing? Faked the data?"

Another sigh. "I don't know, Triz, honestly. Have you talked to Lanniq? His wife is Counterintelligence, so he might know some of her tricks. Then again, I've barely seen him onhab since the, uh." Eir face scrunched. "You know. Arrest thing. He's been picking up extra cockpit time." E and

Triz both looked out at the Skimmer outside, which had rejoined its formation. "We all deal in our own way. No one expected something like that to happen—to any of us, let alone Casne. And pilots always feel more comfortable behind the yoke. You know what that jockey mentality's like, right?"

"*Mentality* implies there's some cognitive activity going on." Triz squinted at the fighters as a tight formation made the outsized Arcwing look more like just another little Swarmer. "From my firsthand experience with cockpit jocks, that's not necessarily the case."

Saabe snorted. "I know the idea probably doesn't appeal right now, but you could try talking to Kalo. I doubt he knows any more of the geeks in Tactics than I do. But he knows Casne. It's worth a shot, isn't it?"

"Maybe," said Triz, so they could part ways more amicably than if she'd dropped a flat no.

* * *

TRIZ'S FEET ACHED. This was a new sensation for her: She was used to cricked necks and sore shoulders from crawling in and around Light Craft all day or hunching over a smaller repair project spread out on a table. When she was younger, much younger, she'd cover half a dozen levels in the Rydoine Hab recycling engines in a single day on her collection routes. But now, just three days of pounding the pathways in the Arcade made her groan. Was she that much fitter then? Or had younger Triz had much more to worry about than sore arches?

In retrospect, taking a break felt like poking a purple bruise to make sure it still hurt. But here she was, in the music-chamber shelter on the Terraria level, body still and head churning. She, Casne, and Nantha liked to come here and relax when they used to be together. Well: Casne and Triz did. Nantha tolerated sitting still for only an hour or two. It was strange to be here without either of them. Before Triz could reconsider, though, an attendant appeared and stooped to set a glass of amber liquid on the low table where Triz had eked out a spot. The birdflute ensemble had seemed like a good bet when she came in here, quiet and peaceful, but maybe she ought to move to the lithogrunge room to drown out the noise in her head. Her fingers closed around the cool glass, and she offered the fob of her other hand for the attendant to scan. "Thanks."

"Of course." Eir collector chirped to complete the transaction. "Just fob-signal when you need a refill."

"Actually . . ." A new voice brought Triz's shoulders up to her ears. "I'll have what she's having, if you don't mind." Kalo dropped to the chaise opposite Triz and flung all four limbs out to maximize his sprawl.

The attendant retreated, either to fulfill this request or to be outside the blast radius of the frustration currently trying to vibrate its way out of Triz.

"What are you doing?" Triz snapped. "We don't have the kind of thing where we sit around drinking and swapping war stories together." They hadn't even done that when they were *together* together—in fact, as she recalled, it was Kalo's chatter about a harrowing engagement with the Ceebees in clusterward space that had precipitated one of their last fights.

"Which is a shame, really, because I have got some *pretty amazing* war stories. But since you're at a bit of a deficit there, it works out."

Triz leaned forward, resting her elbows on either side of

her glass. The flutist was straining his way through the bird-flute's highest range, and every single crisp bright tone drove icepicks into her already-brittle temper. "Already had my share of war stories today. Heard a hell of a one from your Swarmer, actually."

His crooked smile faded, and his gaze slanted down, toward her hands where they pressed against the cold lacquer of the table. "Are you all right? You look like you got dragged through a minefield behind an X-99."

"I'm sure I'll feel better once the view improves." She wanted to put a fist right in the middle of those gappy teeth of his. "Is there something you need, besides attention?"

"Well, yeah." He paused while the attendant set another glass of 'shine on the table between them. "I know you've been trying to track down a sniff of why in the seven hells Casne Veling is behind a Justice wall right now. And I'm a little offended you didn't ask me first."

Triz considered the glass in front of her. She picked it up and turned it around between her fingers. "I figured if you had anything interesting to say, you'd have said it to half the Hab by now. *Did* you see something at Hedgehome?" Anger spiked, and her drink sloshed in its glass. "Are you sitting on evidence that could help Casne and—and trying to make me work for it?"

"Gods of Issam. You seriously think I'd hold back something that would get her out of there?" Kalo took a swig and grimaced. "Never let it be said you don't give it your all. Too bad it's only when it comes to seeing the worst in people."

Triz tossed back the entire glass of 'shine. It burned on its way down, and the burn cooled the fury inside of her. Everyone here sat around wasting time while Casne waited for Justice to turn its back on her. And here was Triz, too, entertaining a space-addled cockpit jock instead of doing the something-real that eluded her. Something that would help Casne. Maybe he'd even been the one to set Casne up, as some sort of ultra-petty revenge for the crash-and-burn of a matchup she'd made between him and Triz. Revenge against either of them, or both, and now he'd come to enjoy a long salty pour of her misery.

Triz couldn't quite square that image with the person she'd—occasionally—enjoyed spending time with. The person who'd brought her confectionary stars from the Webward Pearls, who'd sent her long-distance dinners from halfway across the galaxy when she came down with the strain of mendicant's flu that came through the Hab a few months back. Still, she couldn't rule anything out, even if that made her the ultra-petty one. "What. Do. You. Want."

"To help Casne. I want her out of there too. I mean, do you think she went and grabbed the first pilot she could find to throw at you? She and I *came up* together." That must have meant something in Fleet-talk, because it meant nothing to Triz. "Even if she'd rather crunch numbers than swing a yoke. This is pulling Justice's attention from the Ceebee trials so realistically, Casne's case isn't going to get the attention it deserves. Fleet Hero or not, when a pile of 22CR Starbusters gets unloaded on an occupied Arcology . . . " His throat jerked; Triz looked away. "I'll be your errand boy as long as it means something, the right thing, gets done."

"I tried doing the right thing." Triz beckoned the attendant and pointed at her empty cup. E nodded and took out a larger pitcher to hold up to the 'shine tap. Well. Triz wasn't going to argue with *that.* "It didn't get me anywhere." *And I don't know what to do now*, she didn't add, in case he had an opinion about that.

"Okay, so . . . maybe the right thing is what Casne would do. Or Nantha. And since neither of them is here, and we have to pick up the slack, we have to make do with the Triz thing or the Kalo thing."

"I don't think hitting things with a wrench is going to help. And the Kalo thing is just talking. How's that working out for you so far?"

The attendant set the pitcher neatly on the table; Kalo offered his fob and paid before Triz could. She washed away a muttered thanks with a fresh pour of 'shine. She'd spent a lot already tonight, and she had no job to replenish that credit now. She'd worry about that next. PubWel would see her housed and fed in the meantime anyway.

"You want talk?" Kalo tipped his glass at her. "Fine, let's talk. You know and I know that Casne would never take a shortcut to win a fight." His gaze lengthened, staring through Triz. "I once watched her fight a Ceebee in a dive on Gnosseo without a scrap of tech to help her, just to prove she didn't need it. I've seen her sacrifice her own tactical array to take fire from Do-Ffash pirates so a divvy Hab didn't get hit."

Triz knew about the Fleet's activities clearing pirates out of the Armward Bands thanks to Nantha; she hadn't heard about Gnosseo and had trouble picturing Casne engaged in a fistfight. "She did that?"

"She did. It was amazing. Just . . . don't tell Nantha about that one."

"Tell Miss By-the-Books about a dive bar fistfight? Yeah, I don't think so. She'd probably write a disciplinary note for her own file just for knowing about it." When he grinned, Triz felt a matching expression tug at her own mouth. She crushed that tentative smile under the easy weight of pessimism. "Anyway, yes, we know what we know, that's great. But I don't think any Justice will factor any of that in."

"No, but—don't stop there. So if we know Casne didn't do it, who'd want to smear her?" Kalo slammed his glass down on the tabletop. It tipped onto its side, the round gleaming eye fixed her accusingly. "Lanniq might know some likely suspects, but I haven't seen hide or hair of him in days. He basically lives on the drilling circuit these days. I'm surprised he's not chewing down the Admiral's door himself to get answers. It's not like him to run away from a fight."

"Well . . ." Triz frowned. The two glasses of 'shine blunted the edge of her thoughts. She had to try a few times to pierce Kalo's question about who could be out to get Casne. It felt good, though, like the alcohol could smother the fire of frustration inside her instead of starting a larger conflagration. "The Ceebees, obviously. They'd be mad at her. She was key to their loss at Golros." But *not* because of civilian casualties.

Kalo shrugged dismissively. "Yeah, but they're mad at *a lot* of us. Like, some five thousand Fleet officers and crew. If they were going to fob a war crime off on one of us, why not Savelian, who actually supervised the whole thing?" A curl lifted his lip. "Plus, they have other stuff to be worried about besides revenge, like, I don't know, losing at least half their fleet and their last major planetside strongholds?"

Triz refilled both glasses, then rounded on Kalo. "Why did you ask me what I think if you're going to laugh at whatever I say? Stupid guttergirl with delusions of intelligence."

"I'm not laughing! And I've never thought you were stupid, Triz. You know that. I *hope* you know." His eyebrows came together as she set the pitcher down lopsided and nearly spilled it. "I'm just saying, the Ceebees aren't the big bad monster underneath *every* bed."

"Okay." Her voice rasped when she set her glass down. Like her, it was more than half drained. "You know so much more than the stupid little wrench. Not the Ceebees. Then who?"

"Gods . . ." Both of his hands dug through his hair. "I don't know. A subordinate officer with a grudge. Or a senior officer. Someone living on that Arcology who would rather blow it up than let the Fleet take it back."

Skepticism knit Triz's forehead. "A planetsider who just happened to be stockpiling, uh . . . Starblaster missiles?"

"A few arcologies and Habs out there are built from the wreckage of Fleet vessels!" Kalo argued, but he wilted under the heat of Triz's disdain. "But, no. Not Golros. I'm just saying, the Fleet's whole Fourth Wing defected three years back, and no one knows where they all settled. It's not outside the realm of possibility."

"Sure. But my Ceebee thing is completely wild." Triz poured again but missed her glass. Clear liquid spread across the table and turned it bluish-black. "You don't—you don't have any more idea than me. But you have to act like you do. Don't you?" She shot to her feet, black holes sucking at the edges of her vision.

"Triz, sit down." Kalo pulled at her hand, but she snatched her fingers away. "Shitting stars. I asked if you were okay, I didn't want an object lesson in just how not-okay you are."

The neck of the pitcher offered a reassuring weight to her hand. It would probably make a good weapon, too, if he kept trying to get her to sit back down. "Suck methane, Kalo. I'll handle this on my own."

The noise of the birdflute swallowed Kalo's objections, and the lift doors accepted her without accusation. She lifted the pitcher to her mouth as they started to whisper shut. A hand between the lift doors had triggered the safety stop. When they opened again, Kalo leaned inside. "Hey," he said. "Just let me see you safely home. For old times' sake?"

I don't need any help. I don't want any help. Especially not from you. The words had been in her mouth a moment ago, but it seemed the last of the 'shine had washed them away. "Kalo," she said, and lurched forward. She caught the front of Kalo's uniform before darkness caught her.

CHAPTER SIX

TRIZ WAS—

Awake. Unfortunately.

The bed was cold. Triz groped in the tangled covers for a smooth back, the familiar curve of a shoulder, until the last warm wisps of dream evaporated and she found herself alone. Casne was in Justice, alone, and Triz was—here.

She pushed off her cot with a sticky groan; her tongue clung aggressively to the roof of her mouth while her head pounded an arrhythmic staccato. When she swung her leg out of bed, her bare foot found a puddle. She bent and fumbled around, and came up with an empty pitcher reeking of 'shine. Oh . . . *oh*.

Further examination informed her she was still fully dressed except for her boots and socks. Those waited for her at the end of her bed, just out of reach of the spilled 'shine, fortunately. Triz left them in their place for the time being and emerged from her sleeping chamber for a dearly needed visit to the toilet.

She stopped and her stomach turned.

Kalo was folded up on the tiny sofa in her living area.

He hadn't undressed either, except to take off his uniform jacket and roll it up under his head. In fact, his boots were still on and left dirty marks on the cushion where they rested. Triz put one hand on her clanging head, turned her back on him, and went to pay her dues.

When Triz left the bathroom, Kalo sat up. He spread his jacket out over his lap, trying to knead out some of the deep wrinkles in the fabric. He smiled ruefully at her. "I'd ask if you slept well, but . . ." He shrugged. "Sorry about last night—"

"Shut up." Her lips tightened. "Did we . . . ?"

"Did we? Did we wha—*oh*." He gave his jacket one last shake-out, but his expression had closed off from whatever openness had tried to put itself on offer a moment before.

Seven gods, had she hurt his *feelings*?

"No, I did not take advantage of you in your less-than-optimal state. And good morning to you, too." He turned the inside of his wrist to check his fob. "Good almost-morning. Good I-survived-flight-academy-and-I-still-don't-think-people-should-be-up-this-early-o'clock."

Bile crawled up the back of her throat. She swallowed it but didn't manage to swallow the words that went along with it. She was supposed to be thinking about Casne, Casne who needed her, Casne who was depending on her to put all this right. Casne was who she cared about. But the uncanny familiarity of having Kalo here, in her quarters, had thrown her off-kilter. When she opened her mouth to tell him to go, the wrong words spilled out instead. "What happened at Hedgehome?"

One of his shoulders came up slightly like she'd hit

him. Maybe she *had* finally ended up hitting him with the pitcher last night. "What do you mean, *what happened at Hedgehome*? I've already told you I don't know how that Arcology got destroyed." He knotted his jacket up in his hands again, undoing any progress he'd made in smoothing it out. "I wish I knew, and if I did, I'd blast it from the nearest wallport to every interhab band I could get access to."

"Not Casne. I mean . . ." She leaned back against the bathroom door for support, but it wasn't enough. Her legs bent and she slid to the floor opposite him. "What happened to *you* at Hedgehome?"

He sucked on his front teeth and looked down at his fob. "I can read you the commendation if you want. Let's see: *For meritorious service against overwhelming odds, Kalo Ro-1 Ingte is awarded Allibek's Wings.* I took out nine of theirs, if you were wondering what overwhelming odds entail. Stopped an end-run against the flagship's shieldfault and everything. Barely made it out of medbay after they stitched me back—"

"Show me."

Kalo opened his mouth but caught his tongue between his teeth instead of arguing. He leaned forward and pulled up the hem of his shirt. The wound over his left hip hadn't yet healed, and he winced when Triz crawled across the floor to brush one finger over it. She retreated immediately, but not all the way back to the wall, and he let his shirt drop back into place. How long had she made him stand around and wait in the wrenchworks, with a fresh hole in him? She was so stupid. "You should have *died*," she said, then winced. That wasn't what she'd meant.

But he took no offense. "Got pretty sloppy in there." He shrugged uncomfortably. "Until the air pipes slurped up all the juice." *Juice*. She hated how that sounded. *Blood*. She hated even more how he was looking at her now. "Triz . . ."

"This is stupid," Triz said, and hiccupped. She hadn't realized she was crying, but, well. No putting spilled coolant back in its tube. "I don't want you to die. I wasn't supposed to have to care anymore. You *left* me."

"You'd already left," he said, not unkindly. She looked away. He edged toward her until he could just reach her knee, and patted it sheepishly. She went to knock his hand away, but when her fingers landed on top of his, they stayed there.

"Well, the good news is, uh, I also don't want me to die. Skimmers don't just blow when they're hit like the old Alchemists and Darts used to do, so unless I take a direct hit, the galaxy is more or less stuck with me." The jocularity bled from his voice. He held her knee and said, "I'm not going to ground myself, Triz. I can't do it. Flying is—well, you can't know what it's like if you didn't grow up at the bottom of an Arcology. Nothing but steel for a sky, until you're out there ,and you can go anywhere you want, as fast as you can fly." A rueful grin chipped its way free of the sudden seriousness. "Anywhere you want that you can bend orders to mean, at least. If that's a dealbreaker, it's a dealbreaker, but this is what I do. And I was never going to stop doing it." The grin dried up. "Not even for you."

"Who's asking you to give it up?" She dragged her sleeve across her face and rolled her eyes. "Nothing but steel for a sky," she repeated. "Because of course, growing up inside a recycling engine is nothing but beams of sunshine and, and—rainmows. I mean, rainbows?" She stumbled over the strange word, and Kalo's hand receded.

They were so different. Suns and moons, all over again. But maybe that didn't matter.

"I'm sorry. I didn't mean to launch us into the Divine Trials of the Shitty Childhoods." His elbows rested on his knees, and he leaned forward to rest his head in his hands. "I don't know what I meant to do. I don't know how to pull out of this tailspin. If we could just—"

She didn't give him a chance to spill his latest half-brained idea. She stopped his mouth with hers. Her hands locked onto the collar of his shirt to hold on to the moment just a little longer, before he pulled away and turned this from *maybe* into *absolutely not.*

His hands locked onto her elbows. But instead of pushing her away, he lifted her higher, pulled her against him. Against her lips, he hissed in pain at the sudden movement. He didn't break the contact, though, only held on tighter, his fingers winding into her hair where sleep had loosened it from her braid. "Triz," he said, into the hungry space of her mouth, and she choked on a sob.

Then he did pull away, keeping her close with his hands on her face. She didn't let go of his collar either, wasn't sure her fingers would have uncurled even if she tried. Too many impossible things welled up inside her, and no time to say them all, and no words to say the things she really wanted to, so she blurted the most impossible of all. "I can have your fighter fixed before the tribunes get here. Today even, if I hit it with everything I've got." The minor issue of her unemployment could be resolved when it became a problem. She would break Quelian's fob and lock him in storage if she had to. "You could blow a hole in the top of the Hab and pull her out of Justice. Fly her off to wherever she'll be safe."

"That is—what?" Now he did let go of her, and she sat

down hard on the floor between his feet. "Triz, I can't do that."

"Right. Of course not." Her lips pulled back in a feral snarl, an echo of the expression she'd worn the first time a Tolvian mendicant had cracked open the recycling pits and called down to ask who was in there. A broken shard of light, so very far away, and now, just like then, she was afraid to see what it might show. "I wish I could fly. I'd do it myself. The same way everything gets done around here." She didn't wish she could fly. All that cold black on every side . . . the thought churned her stomach. She hadn't thrown up in the bathroom, but she wasn't ruling out throwing up on Kalo's shirt right now. That offered some small comfort. He reached for her wrist, but she shook him off. "But no, of course not. You can't risk your precious *commission*."

"I can't risk blowing a hole in Justice!" he shouted and it sent a lock of hair into his eyes.

Triz had never heard Kalo raise his voice before. It took the photons right out of her sails, and her shoulders slumped.

When he spoke again, he kept his voice lower, but it came out raw and red as the knotted hurt inside her. "There are other prisoners in there—"

Yeah, Rocan and his Ceebee buddies, missing important appendages.

"Not to mention wardens and clerks. There is no such thing as a safe hull breach. You know better than that."

Triz didn't answer, but she didn't stop him from taking her by the hand this time. They sat like that, tethered together by their limp arms, for several long shuddering breaths. Kalo was the first to break the silence. "If you had something else in the wrenchworks. A Scooper, maybe. Something that'll hold a passenger."

Scoopers usually held crews of two or three and had cargo space to boot. Quelian had several come into the wrenchworks before the Fleet arrived and knocked everything else several slots down their work queues. At least one of them should still be there, probably wanting just a few more hours of attention to get up and flying again. And Quelian wouldn't be down there at this hour. And she would bet a week's pay that he hadn't yet reconfigured the security system to exclude her fob. . . "How are you going to get her out of Justice in a *Scooper*?"

"How am I going to—will you just listen a second?" Kalo let go of her wrist and ran both hands through his hair. "Look. This is not Plan Alpha, Triz. There's going to be a trial, Admiral Savelian will see to it she gets a fair hearing. And any fair hearing is going to clear her name. There's no doubt of that as far as I'm concerned. Okay?"

Before she could open her mouth to spit daggers at him, he kept talking. "But if things go explosive-decompression-style, somehow . . . let's just call it a backup plan. A couple days to get things ready, and get them ready *safely*." As her anger softened, he pressed on: "A Scooper has passenger room, plenty of it, and a fighter doesn't. Now, obviously, I can't scoop a hole out of the top of the Hab. We'll have to figure out a way to get her out of there. There's a drill bit on a Scooper, isn't there? Maybe I could use it to . . . or we could figure out a way to smuggle her to the works . . ."

Belas' face swam up in Triz's vision. "I know someone in Justice who might be willing to help us. It's a *big* might."

"But better than nothing. We'll make it work. Right?"

She didn't answer. Her fingers found his lips and parted

them gently, as if she could pry free the answers she needed. "You'd do that for me?"

"I'd do it for her," he said. "Is that . . . ?"

She stood up, pulling him up by his hand. "It's good enough," she said, and she thought maybe it could be. "Meet me at the wrenchworks tonight. I'll work on Justice today."

"I have an appointment back on the Dailos I can't really miss." Kalo grimaced and Triz made a point not to look while he touched the healing wound through the fabric of his shirt. "If you think of anything I can do from there?"

She wanted to be mad at him for that, for failing to be invincible. But if they were making plans of dubious legality, it might be better to make as small a footprint as possible, so that no one thought to ask the questions to which they wouldn't have the answers. "Tonight, then," she said. She still had his hand in hers, so she gave it an awkward shake before he broke away and retreated from her rooms.

* * *

TRIZ, who'd never been one to turn up her nose at food, forced herself to choke down half a crispbread for breakfast. She poured the spicy sauces from the mealcase into the recycling port—she didn't want to risk anything more than bland bread in her jumping stomach.

Justice didn't open its doors to Hab residents for another hour and change. Counting down the minutes left Triz's patience more brittle than a bad batch of plastisteel. More than once, she stepped up to the door of her pairhome and put her fob to the door to go down to the quad and loop them into this wild plan. Veling would be up for it, and she was a recycling engineer, smart, cool-headed, able to spot the bugs in Triz and Kalo's kludged-up machinations. Casne's damu Othine knew how to fly most of the rigs that came through eir quadhusband's wrenchworks, which would build in some redundancy where Kalo was concerned—not that Triz meant to cut Kalo out of the loop entirely. Or did she? She shelved that question for later. Casne's daddy Idha was quiet but loved his quaddaughter and quadwife enough that, Triz thought, he'd go with Veling on this.

The problem was Quelian. Triz couldn't count on him not to be there, couldn't count on him not catching wind of this somehow. Othine didn't like secrets, e'd spoiled the surprise of Triz's first-ever Remembrance gift before Casne ever gave it to her. Would this be different? Could it?

Each time she got up to go to the door, Triz sat back down. Her cuticles were a bloodied mess by the time her fob alert chirped to let her know Justice's doors had opened.

Queues had already formed by the time Triz emerged from the lift at the top of the Hab. Belas' was long, but she tucked herself into it anyway, behind a man talking loudly into his fob about the indignity of having to pay an import fee for Erreti dry-pearls when he held dual citizenship in one of the arcologies there.

When at last the line shuffled Triz to Belas' counter, he greeted her with a sad smile. "I'm afraid I won't be able to perform the same trick this time. Security is spacetight these days." He lowered his voice. "It'll be on the newschannels tonight, but the Fleet detected an encrypted tight-beam transmission to the Webward Pearls."

"I don't understand. Someone's calling in pirates?" The Pearls had harbored raiders for years, small lightsail gunships that hopped between the system's dozens of miniature moons faster than Fleet fighters could follow. "What does that have to do with Casne?"

"Not her in particular and not pirates at all. The Pearls are where the remnants of Ceebee forces are supposed to have ended up after Hedgehome."

"But all the Ceebees are locked up in . . ." Triz rocked back on her heels. "Someone's smuggling messages out of Justice."

"The Fleet might have some questions for you," Belas said, and shrugged apologetically. His stylus flicked up and down between his fingers, tapping out an anxious rhythm against the countertop. "Considering you paid a visit to Justice recently, under less-than-official circumstances."

"Oh. Yeah, I guess they would." Triz would deal with that when it came up. Along with the fallout from whatever more dangerous plans she enacted in the meantime. She cleared her throat. "I actually came up here to talk to you, though, Belas. I wanted to know, uh . . . what they'll do with Casne if she's convicted. Where she'll go." How they would take her there and who would be holding the keys.

Belas set the stylus carefully down, ending its staccato song. "I have a long queue, Triz. I can't really get into the particulars." He folded his hands. "But if you would like to meet in the Terraria before my shift starts tomorrow morning, I would be happy to explain more to you. The greenery is a very soothing environment for difficult discussions."

And a private one. "Yes. That would be nice. I appreciate it."

"Of course." He gave her a white-lipped smile. "It's been a long time since we've had a chance to just catch up, too, despite being neighbors! I have some pictures my daughter sent me from her new dig site on Sanishar. It's pretty far out

—part of the Sei Worldhold, in fact, so she had to get special diplomatic permission to land there!"

The Sei Worldhold was the nearest government body to the systems of the Confederated Worlds. Triz might be reading too much into Belas' intent expression and oddly stressed words, but hope unfurled inside her, too big and hot to hold for long. She thanked him again, with a tight nod, and fled Justice before she could reach a critical mass of premature optimism.

CHAPTER SEVEN

AFTER THE STATION lights shifted over to Third Shift, Quelian would go back to the quadhome—whatever his own thoughts on the matter, the rest of his gonmates always strictly enforced rules separating work time from home time. Kalo and Triz met at the habitation lift entrance at the appointed time, both dressed in the kind of heavy worksuits ideally suited to illicit undercover Scooper repair. They both stood silently as the lift whisked them downward, carefully looking each other in the boots. Triz racked her aching brain for something to say, anything to break the tension. *Sorry for kissing you last night before asking you to give up your whole life.* Or maybe: *Hey, remember how you almost died two weeks ago, want to give it another shot?* Or better yet—

"So," Kalo said, and Triz jumped. "What happened with that lead of yours in Justice? Not that we're going to need that kind of help, but the gods are more likely to smile on those who prime their engines before launch."

"I'm going to talk to him tomorrow to see if—"

The lift shuddered around them.

Triz fell on her backside on the lift floor, the wind and the rest of the words knocked out of her. Kalo caught himself on the rail, but his head knocked against the lift wall. Triz reached out for him just as the lift lights died.

She counted heartbeats in the pitch black that now surrounded them. Darkness didn't bother her, except when it was a symptom of something much worse. Four, five, six: *there*. Small crackling sounds rippled upward from the floor of the lift to the walls, as emergency release valves deprived of their signals opened. Substrate flooded the tiny tubes lining the edges of the lift, and the bioluminescent bacteria inside got busy. A faint glow began to fill the lift and Kalo's concerned face came into focus.

"What happened?" He spat blood from a split lip. In the soft blue light, his face was strange and unfamiliar, more ghost than man. "We stopped moving?"

"Feels like it." Triz regained her footing and moved to the door. The edges of the doors clung tightly together as she tried to pry them apart. As they were supposed to do to prevent a breach. She grunted in frustration. "I need to see where we are."

"See? I can barely count my fingers in this light."

"Let me save you the trouble." She gritted her teeth and tried to wedge her fingers in between the sealed edge. "There's ten, unless you're even worse at riding a lift than you are flying a Skimmer."

A massive impact rocked the lift on its rotors. Triz scrabbled for purchase against the smooth interior of the lift—what was out there? Even if an undetected asteroid had cleared defenses and hit the Hab, it wasn't as if a storm of space-rocks could be barraging the inside. She put her back against the lift doors and braced for more.

But this time she saw Kalo, limned in blue, kick at the lift railing. The railing gave way, and Kalo ripped it away from the wall. "Thanks for the help counting. Guess you're the brains of the operation. Now move."

She scrambled around him as he jammed one end of the railing into the crack between the doors. His shoulders strained as he levered them apart, inch by inch. "Should you be doing that?" she objected. Head wounds and heavy labor didn't go best hand in hand. But he answered her only with a string of increasingly creative and breathless curses. He didn't drop dead, so she let him work without further comment.

Finally, the doors opened wide enough to hit their safety catches with a series of soft clicks, and Kalo let the broken railing clatter to the floor. "Well, there's air out here, so that's a good sign. Do you think you can get the lift moving again from out there?"

"If the biolights are on, the Hab is running on emergency power." She ticked off the list on her fingers. "Artigrav, water, gas exchange, the umbilicus band, and the bay in the 'works."

He oofed as she elbowed past him and stuck her head out of the lift. "How are people supposed to get around to fix a busted Hab without functional lifts?"

"There's zero-gee access tunnels on the outside of the Hab," she said, feeling around outside the lift doors. "About as accessible as you can hope for with a dark Hab."

"Great. How do we get to one of those?"

"Well . . . we don't." They were between floors, and in the

dark, she couldn't tell which ones. But the lack of a standard door within the limited sight afforded by the blue emergency light suggested they were in the guts of the Hab, the busy organs of life support and gravity generation that lay between the Terraria and the very bottom of the Hab where the wrenchworks lay. All right. She could work with that. This was going to be . . . interesting. "They're built into the skin of the Hab. We're pretty much right in the middle of the thing."

"So we wait here hoping, till someone turns the lights on?"

"Not exactly." She pointed at the lift. "*You* wait here in the lift. I'm going to see how far I can get." And she squeezed out between the lift doors and the lift chute.

Behind her, Kalo sputtered in pointless alarm, but the rungs of a narrow maintenance ladder gave her handholds and footholds. Once she cleared the top of the lift car, she reached out in the darkness of the chute and groped against the cold walls. There: another ladder. She stretched her leg and moved sideways. Two more lateral movements brought her to the cold, hard opening of a hatch, slightly recessed into the wall. "Here we go," she muttered, just as a grunt signaled Kalo's arrival on the chute ladder. She aimed a lancet-sharp glare into the blackness where the sound had come from. "I told you to wait in the lift!"

"Well, if we're going to be technical, I'm still in the lift. Just not the lift *car*. What are we doing out here, and how long are we going to be doing it? I'm not keen on being up here when the lift comes back into service."

"*If* it comes back," she said, and they both hung onto the side in silence for a moment. Then she reached for the hatch handle. "You're not going to like this." The handle resisted her one-handed efforts to turn it. She squeezed one arm through the nearest rung of the ladder so she could reach the handle with both hands. It groaned and then grudgingly gave way. The hatch wasn't open far before a pungent odor hit Triz squarely in the face.

Kalo gagged. "I'm afraid to ask what it is we're smelling and even more afraid to ask why we can smell it."

Triz pushed the hatch open and took one last almost-bearable breath in the lift chute. "The hero of Hedgehome is about to become the hero of Recycling Engine 2b." Her hands found purchase inside the slightly slick opening behind the hatch, and she pulled herself forward to get both knees inside. Crawling on her hands and knees in the wet darkness, she turned back to call over her shoulder. The rising mucus in her throat made her voice thick. "Or you can go back to the lift and wait for either the Hab to come back online or your own death. Whichever comes first."

"Both appealing compared to what's in there." A dull metallic thud and a shadow in the tunnel blotted out what remained of the emergency lights in the lift chute. "Well, this is your turf. Where to?"

Triz's fingers found an opening in the floor ahead of her, a space where the impenetrable blackness grew even blacker. She grimaced. At least she knew what to expect down there. "Follow me," she said, and Kalo's exclamation of dismay echoed after her as she pulled herself feet-first into the tube and began to shimmy downward.

* * *

THE SMELL GREW STRONGER and viler by the time they reached the bottom of the shaft and dropped down with a splatter into a chamber full of soft, slick organic foodwaste.

When Triz struggled to her feet, the sludge reached past her ankles. "Could be worse," Triz said, and suppressed a gag. It really could be; there were big piles of organic waste stacked up beneath some of the disposal chutes. She might just have easily landed in the middle of one of *those*.

A strange pride rose up in her, along with her gorge, at the ability she'd retained being able to manage in this kind of place. On its heels, a disturbing thought: all these years later and she was still a guttergirl at heart. She peeled a flat, sticky piece of ex-spicefruit off her backside, a bit pointlessly, and let it drop back into the muck. "Can you keep moving?"

"Whatever gets us out of here faster." He coughed. "The smell notwithstanding, the faster we can find out what's wrong with the Hab, the better."

Triz stopped so fast he walked into her back. "The faster we can spring Casne, you mean. This might be our best shot to get her out of Justice."

"Are you serious?" He grabbed for her sleeve, but she wriggled out of his grip and scrambled down to a low point in the heap of food scraps. Her feet found the bottom of the next mountain of slop, and she started edging upward and forward as he called after her. "At best, the central power conduits are out of commission, at worst the whole station's fried. Ambient energy's getting drained every second keeping this place flush with oxygen, and there might be fifty thousand people to evacuate on just *three* shitting whaleships."

"You think no one upstairs is working on that? We have our own problems to worry about." She slipped on a soft spot and landed wrists-deep in sludge. "I need to find the port into Metal Reclamation."

"I'm not convinced there's anyone upstairs with the authority and-or know-how to worry about that." He paused and groped in the dark for the back of her jacket; she switched on her fob's spotlight to give them something to see by. "Can I just say, I can't believe you lived in one of these."

"Lots of kids do, on the big Habs like Rydoine. Probably on the bottom levels of planets like Ro, too. Anywhere people get packed in so tight that they don't notice who falls through the cracks. Or care. And you get used to the smell." That last was barely a lie. You couldn't completely turn off the part of your brain screaming *this is not normal, this is bad, this is wrong,* even if you'd been mucking your entire life. Triz was born in the sludge and before the Tolvians found her she expected to die in the sludge. But gutterkids learned to ignore that little niggling voice, at least if they wanted to eat another day.

She tripped, and realized the echo of their movements had changed: a muting of their clangs and muttered curses. Something had shifted in the shape of their echoes . . .

Oh, no. Triz stilled, listening. But she felt the dull distant vibrations, rolling up from the floor through her bones, before her ears caught it. *Of course.* Listening with your feet was an old gutterkid trick; how had she ever managed to forget it? "We need to hurry up."

Kalo made a retching sound. "No arguments here."

"No, I mean, we *really* need to hurry up." Triz was half-groping, half-running through the sludge now. "Do you hear that?"

"Nine arms of—" He stilled, trying to get a hold of the noise. "Is that the turning arm?"

"Got to pulverize and aerate the waste," Triz gasped, pawing her way forward. "Come on and help me look unless you want to get shredded!"

"I don't even know what we're looking *for.*"

"A vent, there's supposed to be a vent here somewhere—"

"What did you used to do when turning happened back when you lived in one of these things?"

"Avoided it."

They struggled side by side through the muck. They were up to their knees now; higher for Triz, and the sludge had developed a distinct current that threatened to suck them under. She screeched when she slipped, and Kalo caught her by the elbow before she got a faceful of antique food. "It's getting louder!" he shouted in her ear.

"*I know.*" Even over the growing hum of the turning arm, her raised voice had echoed oddly. She shifted the light from the fob, turning to her left, it illuminated a stained, pitted wall. "Ha!"

Kalo wiped his face on the shoulder of her jacket, for all the good that would do him. "Please tell me we can get out of here now."

"I think so. Give me a hand." He bent his knee, and she planted a foot on it to push upward. When she walked her fingers along the wall above and to her right, the sharp edge of a vent bit into her finger. "Ouch!"

"*Triz*—" When she flicked the fob light out over his head, she could see the faint outline of the turning arm, whipping through the sludge, grinding spicebread rinds and bioplast wrappers to a pulp.

"Here we go."She pulled the vent cover free and pulled herself upward with help from Kalo, who scrabbled up close behind with only the assistance afforded by a prolific stream of curses. Once they both made it into the vent duct, they lay still, not quite touching. When the turning arm passed, it splattered them—mostly Kalo—with a last layer of organic gunk. One final indignity.

Finally, after they'd caught their breath, Kalo crawled forward, elbows ringing hollowly against the bottom of the vent, and laid his forehead against her knees. "Gods. Let's definitely never compare shitty childhoods again because you win, now and forever."

She ran one hand through his hair and cast aside a greasy strand of organic who-knew-what. "You ready for Metal Reclamation?"

"Does it smell better in there? Then, please, lead the way. We've got a Hab to save."

"A friend to rescue, I think you mean," Triz corrected. "Whatever's happening, I think it bumps rescuing Casne up to Plan Alpha."

"Triz—"

"The Ceebees have got to be behind this." It wasn't a question, but his silence answered her anyway. "If nothing else, we need Casne's help to stop whatever it is they've planned. Unless you're a strategy master, as well as fighter jock now, and just didn't think to mention it." With some effort, Triz turned in the narrow space to bring her boots up against the plastic vent on the far side. She bent her knees, then paused. "I should warn you, the Reclamation electrobacteria might damage your fob. They're hungry little monsters."

"Oh—um, sure." Kalo stumbled a little over the sudden change in conversational direction. "Well. I guess fobs aren't going to be a lot of help to us anyway as long as the Hab's gone dark. And . . ." A slight scuffling in the duct behind her. "Will they eat any other metal bits on me, I guess? Like, uh." He hesitated. ". . . Boot grommets?"

"If your shoes come untied I'm *not* carrying you." Triz struck hard against the plastic and pushed the broken pieces out of the way with her feet. A glimmer of light painted the jagged opening a sickly green; some devices must have been recycled without being properly powered down first. They still used the Hab's ambient energy to uselessly light the dark as they waited for Reclamation. Triz edged down into Metal Reclamation and landed atop a chair, which may have been broken before her arrival but which certainly was after. "Ow!"

"Nice place. Great vibes." Kalo dropped down just behind her, crushing a pile of corroded parts. "Let's open an art gallery down here."

Triz began pushing piles of rusty metal out of the way, trying to clear some space on the floor. She grunted as a hulking, antiquated model of food printer resisted her efforts. "A little help here?"

"Not a gallery? Okay, you're thinking maybe a poetry salon." He put his shoulder to the printer, and it screeched across the floor in answer to his efforts. A rough edge caught his hand as he straightened; he wiped blood on his trousers. "We looking for anything in particular, or are you just collecting spare parts?"

"A hinge. Or a seam of some kind." Triz felt around the open space and found nothing but smooth paneling. "There's a secretion apparatus built into the bottom of Reclamation, where we get wiring and plates extruded into the wrenchworks as we need them. Of course, it breaks about once a cycle, so there's a way to open the whole thing up for repairs. It's plenty big enough for us to get into the works through there." She groped around into the middle of another pile and came up with a shimmerlamp whose silvery orb still gleamed faintly. She'd found one in the recycling pits as a kid, and successfully defended it in her hoard for a few years before it got crushed by an unscheduled run of that engine's aeration stir. "It might even let your ego through, with a bit of squeezing."

"The hero of Hedgehome does not squeeze." He kicked over a pile of wall panels, which collapsed into a gnarled knot of pipework with a terrific clatter. But something in the wreckage made him stoop for a closer look, and he ran one boot back and forth in the little clearing. "Hey, this seems promising."

Triz helped him shovel back metal remnants to open a space a meter across. "This is it!" She wedged her fingers into the seam and winced as it resisted her attempts to force it apart. "Can you help me pry it open?"

He got one hand into the gap she'd opened and levered it wide. Inside was a tangle of pipes and parts. Triz groped around it, freeing what pieces of the extrusion apparatus she could remove by hand. While she separated parts from their fittings, Kalo paced. "You're abnormally quiet," she said, after a few minutes' work. "Should I be worried?"

"Please don't be. If you're worried about me, then I'll know something's really wrong. I'm just—" The sentence trailed off in an embarrassed laugh. "It's, uh. Not working." He flapped his left hand once, then let it hang limp at the end of his wrist.

Triz stared at him, trying to guess at his expression through the shadows. His sense of humor didn't always match hers, but she didn't think he was joking now. "Your hand isn't working? What am I supposed to do with a one-handed pilot? You only cut it . . ."

On a sharp edge in Metal Reclamation.

Where electrobacteria chewed up anything metallic in sight.

She shined the light in his face; he put his arm up to shield his eyes. She wanted to see his face. "Your hand isn't working," she echoed. *Because it's made of metal. Like a Ceebee.*

CHAPTER EIGHT

"I'M STILL SPACEWORTHY," Kalo said, as if she'd somehow done something to offend *him*. A deep breath cooled the fire of Triz's outrage. She didn't have time to be angry right now, or to unpack his hurt feelings, real or feigned. *Casne* didn't have time. She found the access panel and punched her way through. It screeched on its hinges as it swung down into the wrenchworks. Triz followed it, boots first.

It took Kalo another moment to land behind her in the dark wrenchworks. The emergency lighting gleamed eerie blue here, too, turning the stranded Swarmers into pale ghosts of their former glory. Other systems had come online, though: This far at the end of the Hab from the primary ambient generators, the 'works had a few systems important enough to warrant redundant emergency power sources of their own. A faint dry breeze wafted down from the air vents, and the amber operation light shone beside the huge airlocks at the center of the 'works. That loosened the tight set of Triz's jaw a little.

As Triz surveyed the situation, the wallport lit up, its screen crawling with red and yellow warning symbols. A good sign. The maintenance crews uphab must be busy. She crossed to the wallport and offered her fob, which clicked once and promptly died. It, too, had lost its integrity to the bacteria in Reclamation. She unlatched the manual keypad from its node and typed in her own queries. She didn't look up when Kalo approached, but resentment crawled out between her clenched teeth anyway. "So, you're a Ceebee."

"Gods of—do they have exclusive rights to mods? There's billions of people in the Confederated Worlds and most of them have one augment or another."

He hadn't actually answered her accusation. She met his bluster with stony silence.

He exhaled noisily. "*No*, Triz, I'm not a Ceebee! Or if I am, I'm a pretty awful one, considering how many of them I blasted out of the sky at Hedgehome. You think I'm the only pilot with nano repairs? Or combat mods?" He sat down against the wallport, smearing a sticky trail of muck down the wall. "Being a Ceebee isn't about what you do to yourself. It's about what you do to other people to get what you think you deserve. So tell me, Triz, what exactly do I deserve?"

Triz bit her tongue. She didn't know whether he was lying to her and didn't have the stomach to figure it out now, to hold up the pieces side by side, and see where they matched up. Someone wanted Casne's career ended, someone close to her who had the opportunity, motive, Fleet access . . .

She couldn't make the shapes fit the Kalo she'd known,

so she didn't try and keyed in a query to the family quad-home instead. The call rang and rang and rang unanswered, so she tried another query. This time, she put in a request to an unmanned wallport terminal upstairs in the Arcade. "What are you doing?" Kalo asked. She ignored him, and he let his head fall back against the wall behind him.

Mercifully, this time it pinged a response, and she keyed in her passcode for access. When she needed to do her weekly shopping, she'd always liked to use an open Arcade port to make sure the crowds weren't packed around the fungus vendors and the nutrient tankers. Maybe she could use the same method now to get a glimpse of the situation upstairs. Better yet, someone might notice the in-use port and actually *tell* her what in all the worlds was going on in the Hab. And whether whatever was going on uphab might be going on in Justice too. If Kalo couldn't handle it, maybe she could fly the Scooper herself? How hard could an old ore hauler be to fly?

She grasped at the tenuous fragments of that fantasy as the screen flickered, then resolved. Or almost resolved; Triz squinted and tried to make sense of what she saw.

After a moment, the image came together in her brain as well as on the screen. It was the Arcade she knew, but scribbled over in lines of gnarled green-brown. White lines flashed back and forth and left lingering visions on the port screen. Triz asked for volume and received it. The shrill hum of the white lines sliced through her. After a moment, a pair of lancet guns barked in answer.

Kalo's chin lifted off his chest. "What was that?"

She gestured to the screen, wordless.

He whistled low. "Tunnelguns."

That word Triz recognized. Tunnelguns were Ceebee

stuff, the technology still beyond what the Fleet's exotics-wranglers had been able to come up with. And probably more unpredictable than what the Admiralty would have tolerated in service anyway. "That green shit must be one of their bioweapons," Triz murmured. The Hab's immunodefenses *should have* stopped any kind of bioweapon, Triz wanted to say, but *should haves* didn't patch the plastiglass.

Kalo was already on his feet. "Rocan," he said, and cursed. "Rocan has to be behind this. Someone helped him escape Justice." He looked around wildly. "I need a fighter. Get me in the most spaceworthy one you've got."

"What?" That tore her attention from the wallport. "To stop him or to save him?"

He rounded on her, his bad hand held close to his chest, bent at an unnatural angle that indicated it was missing some significant metal-based infrastructure. "Shitting stars, Triz! You want to have, what, an ethical debate on biomods right this second?"

Arguments died in her throat. This was Kalo she was talking about. What an awful thing, to accuse someone she'd . . . *cared about* of being a Ceebee. "I'm sorry," she said, trying to mean it. His shoulders pulled taut. "I don't—I don't understand, and I can work on that later, but what I want right this second is to make sure Casne's safe."

His stiff posture slackened a little and the hard tendon in his jaw softened. "Getting me in a light attack Swarmer right now gets you a step closer to that."

"There's two whaleships at anchor outside! Let their swarms handle it."

He gestured violently to the port. "They don't know he's on the loose with a Ceebee rendezvous on the way, but *we* do."

"I think you're overlooking one shitting detail. What are you going to fly with? Your *feet*?"

"I'll figure something out." He was already stomping toward the row of moribund Skimmers and Arcwings, stepping over the coils of loose tubing and ducking under the tangles of wires that dragged out of open panels. "This one doesn't look half bad." He pointed, hand flapping.

Triz threw her arms in the air. "It *looks* fine because we pulled the entire arc array out of it for refitting. We were stomping all over its guts in Metal Reclamation ten minutes ago. Leave it be."

A flicker of activity tugged Triz's eyes back to the wallport. Two figures cut their way across the Arcade, in her view. The one taking cover behind must be Rocan. The Ceebee commander's eyes weren't mere holes anymore: even at the distance afforded by the wallport, Triz saw the faint gleam of some kind of misbegotten tech. The translucent outline of exotic-based body armor draped the shoulders of both men like a cloak, only flaring into full light when a lancet burst came close.

The second man . . . looked like Lanniq?

That didn't make any sense.

Triz frowned at the strange sight and tried to remember what she'd been saying. "The only thing close to ready is the Scooper I told you about. Kalo, I think Rocan is on the move. And . . ." Confusion bit off her words. She'd already seen the damage done by a misplaced accusation. Shitting stars, she'd done a little damage herself just now. But this time, she didn't think her eyes had lied to her. "And I think he's got Lanniq with him running cover."

"Lanniq?" Kalo spun on one heel and almost tripped over a vacuum casing. "No. He hates the Ceebees. His nephew joined them, and Lanniq never heard from him again."

"See for yourself." Triz gestured at the port screen so violently she almost missed the flash of movement. Not a barrage of lancet fire. Just one body in Fleet gray that dropped onto Lanniq from the Arcade level above. Triz's heart beat a ragged double-time.

Casne. Casne, why?

Casne's legs scissored between Lanniq's and sent him sprawling. She ripped his antilancet cloak away from him, but a vicious kick knocked her rolling several paces. Triz gasped. When Lanniq ran to meet her head-on, she was on her feet waiting, and he seemed to see her for the first time. Whatever words passed between them were lost in the chaos. Then, a flash of movement behind Casne: Rocan's palm, turning upward toward her.

A scream of warning died in Triz's throat.

The tunnelgun hidden inside Rocan's wrist fired.

Casne took a step forward. Triz couldn't say which happened first, until the white lines cleared from her vision, and she saw Casne tumbling head over foot toward the new hole in the Arcade perimeter. A hole opening into space.

"No," Triz heard herself say softly.

That tiny figure was framed in the space of the hole for just a moment, a perfect X. A shimmer at the neck: Casne's Tactics collar insignia catching a shard of light.

Then the limp doll of a Justice officer's body slammed into Casne, and they both blinked out of existence. Only a black hole left where Casne had been, with starlight flickering like funeral lights in the void.

"No," Triz said, "no, no, she can't, no." She couldn't feel

her face; her teeth clipped her tongue, and her mouth filled with blood, but it didn't hurt. It felt like drowning.

She couldn't look away from the wallport. Lanniq and Rocan strained, their feet held securely against the metal plates of the deck. Mag boots—or Mag feet, perhaps, in Rocan's case. She couldn't see Lanniq's face, but Rocan's was expressionless, intent only on their destination across the Arcade.

The lift tubes.

They still have reserves hidden out there, Saabe had argued. *Maybe somewhere webward of Golros.*

The Fleet detected an encrypted tight-beam transmission to the Webward Pearls, Kalo had told her.

And he'd asked her for a fighter . . . oh.

The Ceebees were coming to collect their wayward leader.

So Lanniq and Rocan were heading for the lift to climb down to the wrenchworks. Of course they were, because the wrenchworks was their ticket out of the Hab. Rocan would never be able to swim an umbilicus tube fast enough to make it to a rescue ship before the whaleboats mustered their Light Attack Swarms to intercept. But a fast, small ship could enter via the wrenchworks airlock and be gone again before the whaleships could react.

When Triz blinked, the broken pieces of her rescue fantasy cut the insides of her eyelids. "I'll get you a ship," Triz said, and blood ran down her chin. Casne would have known what to do now. Maybe Kalo would too.

But when she looked over her shoulder, he was gone.

CHAPTER NINE

OF COURSE HE WAS GONE. Kalo was always going to be gone at some point, and that was why this shitting quad could never be. He was half man and half precarious quantum state teetering on the edge of collapse. Erased from existence by the barrage of a ground array's superheater? Or beating a retreat from responsibility and sentiment and grief? Gone was gone.

Triz picked up her wrench. It didn't matter what Casne would do, or what Kalo would say. She wasn't either of them. And she knew what she needed to do now. She didn't know how long it would take Lanniq and Rocan to climb down the length of the Hab, though with a tunnelgun in their possession, she guessed they wouldn't suffer the indignity of having to traverse the recycling engines.

She had to get a ship working. One boot in front of the other. If there was no one else in position to intercept Rocan's rescue, then she would have to do it herself. Sure, she'd never flown a ship before, but she'd been in one so many times, hadn't she? Albeit on this side of the Hab bay doors. How different could it be to take this thing into space? Her stomach pitched queasily. She took a different tack: imagining how satisfying it would be to apply the drill bit to the hull of whatever Ceebee ship dropped out of space to make the pickup.

Her wrench bit down on a bolt. Two dust-clogged filters to replace, and this Scooper would be spaceworthy. Just two. Her wrist turned, her arm strained. It felt good to work. Working, at least at this stage of the process, did not require thinking. Only doing.

A dirty filter hit the floor and coughed up rust-red powder. Triz kicked it aside and hefted a clean one. It clicked neatly into place. Triz liked things in their place. So did Casne. Triz's pairhome had always been neater than the rooms shared by Casne's quadparents. It was comfortable to nestle, for a moment, in the warmth of memory. Too comfortable. In memory, Casne was still alive. Triz's eyes watered, but she fastened the filter back into place and reached for the second one.

It was something, to have been witness to Casne's final moments. An act of bravery. Never the cowardice they'd accused her of. She'd tell Veling and the other quadparents. Quelian too. She'd scream it into his face if he wouldn't listen. She thought he would. She'd make him.

The second panel popped into place, and it occurred to Triz none of Casne's quadparents might've survived her. She didn't know how much of a hole the tunnelgun had created in the Hab. Obviously, support systems were still running, but it was entirely possible Rocan had shot through the part of the Hab where people lived. She closed the open wound in the Scooper's side and probed the oozing sore of the possibility of an entire quadhome erased in an hour's bloody work. No. She had to believe they were still alive, that Rocan's main goal was getting here, to this wrenchworks.

And Nantha. Oh, no. She could imagine telling Casne's mother what happened, their knees close together and hands twisted into two-tone knots. But her wife, who had made her home in Casne's heart and occupied so many of the warm hollow spaces in Triz's too? She didn't have words for that.

The Scooper was finished. Triz stood up and looked at her hands. She'd raised a blister on the heel of one thumb. It would heal. It would have to. She needed to fill the fuel tanks. She needed to work faster.

The soft patter of falling water reached her ears. The sound stopped her completely.

Her head turned toward the wrenchworks office, and her body followed. She stepped over Kalo's wadded shirt on the floor, his trousers, his boots. The fading emergency lights lit the office a dull blue; she pushed on the half-closed door to the staff shower, where Kalo sat beneath the spray. He might've been here the whole time she worked. It was closed-circuit water, devoted to the works, so there was no ration to use up. But he must have used up the remaining heat without the ambient generators flowing to power the heating elements: his skin was raised in gooseflesh.

So he didn't leave after all.

"Kalo. Get out of there."

"I thought of rescuing Casne before you did, you know. Not with a starfighter, just on my own two feet. Shooting my way into Justice like the hero in a bad 'port drama." He turned his hands palm upward; one collected water, while droplets cascaded down the slack one. "If I'd had the conviction to act right away . . ."

"You'd probably be in a Justice cell yourself. Or maybe you'd be dead too." Dead. That word jumped in Triz's mouth. It made things too real, brought them in from their safe distance. She edged forward, put herself under the icy spray of the shower. The cold cut her to the bone, and the water washed away the things she couldn't handle yet. One thing at a time. And at *this* time, she needed a pilot.

At this time, she needed someone who wasn't gone.

She put her arms around him and shared his shivering. The elbows of her shirt wept dirty water. Triz didn't cry. She wasn't ready to open that reservoir yet. It ran deep, and she didn't want to look at the things lurking below the surface. She'd already mourned once, for the Casne who was unjustly arrested; she couldn't plumb those depths afresh already. She reached over her head and turned the water shutoff. "Kalo," she said. She put her hand on his neck; he lifted his head and met her eyes. "We need to move."

He complied and climbed to his feet. Some vestige of military discipline kicking in. They found spare clothes in the crew lockers. Triz dressed in her own clean tunic and leggings; she rifled through the others' things to produce something usable for Kalo. He shrugged into one of her old shirts, which stretched too tight across his shoulders, and cinched a pair of Quelian's sagging pants about his waist. There was nothing for it but to shove his feet back into his own sodden boots. "Are you spaceworthy?" she asked, and his chin jerked in a nod. "Good."

From the wrenchworks proper, a rhythmic banging echoed its way to them. Triz stiffened; Kalo's head came up. "Rocan," he said, and he was already striding toward the door.

Before he left the office, Kalo's good hand went to an

empty pocket where a Fleet sidearm might usually rest. He looked over his shoulder at Triz, and if he was afraid, it didn't show on his face. "Stay here. I'll take care of this."

"What are you going to do, slap him to death?" Triz swallowed irritation with an undercurrent of anxiety and shoved in front of him so she alone occupied the office doorway. She craned her neck for a better view of the wrenchworks. "Besides, I'm not so sure it's him." Kalo made an irritated noise and wedged himself between her and the door. The sound repeated itself: the same pattern of knocks she'd heard the first time. "That wasn't coming from the lift, it was coming from . . ."

"The airlock," he finished. He slammed her arm aside and crossed the works at a dead run before she knew what was happening.

"Wait!" He was already keying in an order at the terminal at the base of the works. Beneath Triz's feet, the floor hummed and jumped as mechanical gears ground together. The outer airlock was dilating, and gods only knew what lay on the other side. "What are you doing? If there's a Ceebee entry team out there, we don't stand a chance."

"It's not an entry team." The humming beneath Triz's feet stopped briefly, then began cycling again. Closing the outer doors, pumping air into the sealed chamber. She stepped back from the lock, avoiding the lifttrain that would have hefted whatever wounded ship waited inside. Maybe a canister of spray sealant could function as a makeshift weapon—if she could find a hose she could spray it in an unguarded face—

The inner doors dilated with a hiss of cold, misty air. Kalo dropped to his belly at the widening rim. "Give me your hand," he said, and thrust one arm, his good one, down into the lock. Five space-dark fingers with frost-spangled stars closed around his wrist.

Triz's heart leaped sideways in her chest. She ran across the works and left skin on the decking where she threw herself down beside Kalo. Casne clung one-handed to Kalo's arm: She must have jumped from the bottom of the lock ten feet below. Triz stretched with both arms and Casne flung her free hand up to grab a second hold. Her fingers were so cold they burned, but Triz didn't care. Casne's boots paddled the misty air, but she cranked her head back to find Triz. Ice rimed her face. Her frozen features were split into a stupid grin.

Triz's throat spasmed. "I could've gotten a ladder if you'd waited one shitting minute." Her arms strained, Kalo grunted, and then they were moving back as Casne's boots found purchase on the lip of the airlock. For a moment, they all stared at each other, sprawled flat-out on the deck. Then Casne lunged forward to tackle them both with arms spread wide.

Her skin still burned where it touched Triz, and when it burned, it drove waves of breathless smoky laughter out of her, all the grief she had shoved down and put aside converted to impossible, ever-expanding joy. They were all laughing, less giddy than hysterical, and when the laughter guttered and ran dry, they only clung to each other. As if making up for lost time, and Triz had lost so much time already. As if letting go would make the image unravel like a 'port drama gone off the rails.

When Triz had the breath to ask the impossible question, she did. "How did you survive?"

"I'm modded, Triz. And I was lucky to have my Fleet boots on in my cell. They magnetize when they detect depressurization. Never out of uniform, right?" Casne's half-smile faded. The press of fingers and lips had erased some of the rime from her face, but hazy nebulae still mottled her forehead. She rubbed her forearms with her hands and looked at Kalo, who shrugged and avoided Triz's eyes. "I know you don't like the idea, but combat adaptations save lives."

"I'm coded for conditional production of cold resistance proteins too," Kalo said, to the deck. "And infected with hypoxia-activated Aerobacter. Only reason I'm still flying."

Triz rubbed her wet eyes. "I'm not—I'm glad you're alive, Cas!" She could barely *believe* it, but she was glad. "I thought . . . I don't know what I thought. That once you crossed the line between human and Ceebee, you'd just keep crossing lines." Casne and Kalo flicked a gaze at one another. "But I guess it's not really that simple."

"That's a good way to start thinking about it," said Casne, at the same time Kalo said, "Well, seeing as I haven't tried terraforming an alien intelligence out of existence to build myself a castle, yeah."

They all three laughed.

Before the lift doors exploded.

CHAPTER TEN

TRIZ'S EARS RANG. She lifted her hands from her head. No sign of Casne and Kalo beside her. No! She'd just gotten Casne back; she couldn't lose her again. She struggled to her knees, then her feet, and looked around.

She could still hear human voices under the shrill of the ringing, but they seemed so terribly far away. Muffled by the yellow-gray smoke drifting through the works, maybe.

Smoke? In the wrenchworks?

Triz spun. The smoke billowed out from the blistered lift doors. And amid the conflagration, four figures traded blows.

Casne. Kalo. Lanniq. Rocan.

Casne fought with Lanniq for control of a lancet gun. Kalo forced Rocan's tunnelgun, buried where his wrist and hand should be in his flesh, down just in time for a blast to slice through the nearest Skimmer. The fighter canted sideways, misbalanced by the weight of the slice of missing fuselage that crashed to the floor in the opposite direction. When the fighter struck the deck, it rattled Triz's teeth, but she barely heard the sound. She was focused on the two people in front of her, the two pieces of her heart battling for their lives. Even to her untrained eye, both Casne and Kalo moved slower than Lanniq and Rocan, muted by exhaustion and injury.

Lanniq swept Casne's feet out from under her and the lancet gun went skittering across the floor.

Kalo dove for it, and the tunnelgun cut a long narrow swath through the floor between him and the weapon. This one bled darkness—space and dark matter—before the unstable tunnel faltered and closed off, leaving only a ragged, smoking canyon in the deck.

That could easily have been a hull breach if Rocan's aim had been a little higher. The others might survive a breach if they were lucky. Triz wouldn't.

Triz grabbed for the sealant canister she'd dropped before. She caught it by the hose and dragged it along behind her. If Rocan breached the hull again—if he aimed faster or better this time—

Rocan spun to meet Triz. He didn't raise the tunnelgun embedded in his wrist toward her. Maybe it needed to recharge? He came toward her, snarling. Rage glinted in his eyes—the silvered marble of his right implant, and the dull gray of the left, which must have been damaged in the melee. Triz stumbled back, but he was on her, and his elbow met her sternum with startling precision. She doubled over in silent paroxysms. Rocan seized her hair and slammed her face into his knee. Stars exploded red and gold behind her eyes, and she swung the sealant blindly as she fell. It connected with something, not Rocan, and spun out of Triz's hand. Rocan's knee hit Triz's chin this time and split her lip.

The lancet gun cried out a warning.

Something heavy struck Triz hard. She fell with it. Her head rebounded off the deck; her mouth opened around a yelp, but she had no air in her lungs to give it voice. Blood dribbled down the back of her throat. She scrabbled to get the weight off of her chest, her legs, but it was so heavy she was so afraid of what she'd see when the daze of stars lifted. This was it, then. That's what she got for trying to claw her way out of the gutter.

"Triz!" The pressure lifted off Triz slowly, then all at once, and Kalo's hands were on her. "Shitting, shitting stars." He ripped open her jacket, ran fingers over her chest and belly and down her legs. "Are you hit? I shouldn't have taken the shot. It was too close."

The deck shuddered beneath them. Kalo dropped Triz and looked around wildly. "He was *just* here!" he said, and whirled around as Triz's freshly fixed Scooper rose into the air of the bay and then lurched forward off its blocks.

"Rocan!" Kalo cried, and ran across the wrenchworks.

Triz turned back to the lifeless body beside her. She stared stupidly at Lanniq, whose lifeless eyes were fixed on a point somewhere above. Human eyes, not like Rocan's. Triz's hand found his shoulder, and she shook it, hard. He didn't respond. She took off her jacket and tried to blot the blood welling up on his shirt. Why was she trying to help him? She didn't know. She felt the floor hum as the airlock dilated, though all she could hear was Kalo's scream of frustration.

"Triz." Casne again, her voice a distant tinny shout. She crawled over to Triz and took her hands off Lanniq. Triz drank in the sight of Casne's face, pinched with pain but still whole. "He's gone." Triz dropped the jacket, and Casne tugged it over Lanniq's staring face. The fabric draped over the mass of lancets embedded in his chest, too. "He took the shot for Rocan."

Triz dragged her hand across her chin, and her wrist came away streaked in scarlet. "I thought he hated the Ceebees." Her hearing had started to return, shaken loose by the blunt hammering of her own voice against the insides of her ears. "Why die for one?"

"I don't know." Casne's tone hardened. "But I can guess. He wouldn't be the first Fleet officer they've compromised." Casne tried to stand, but her right leg wobbled. Triz realized what she'd hit with the sealant canister.

"That missing nephew," Casne said. "If he led the Cyberbionautic Alliance to Lanniq's triad? Instantly compromised officer." Her jaw jutted out as she looked over Lanniq's still body.

Triz wondered what Casne would have done in the same situation.

Kalo loped back alongside them. "I need a ship, and fast," he said without preamble. "Rocan's got the Scooper."

"The Scooper." Triz rubbed her eyes. "Right. He won't get far, not very fast. Scoopers aren't built for speed."

"We thought the Ceebees were coming here to collect him. But he must need to make it to a rendezvous point . . . which means he's expecting a pickup waiting somewhere close by." Kalo's feet shuffled on the deck as if he would have liked to simply run Rocan's Scooper down. "Get me in any fighter that'll hold atmo."

"Kalo, I don't have anything spaceworthy to give you. The next closest thing to ready is still just a Tiresh with a misfiring injector, and it's not like you can fly it while I've still got it up on the blocks—" She bit her tongue to cut that idea short. Best not to put a thought in Kalo's head before she could work out all the implications. Implications like: Triz, in the fragile canopy of a Light Attack ship, out in the big black.

But Casne beat her there. "The Tiresh-15 is a four-man gunship. Could you pull open the ventral engine from inside and, and . . ."

Triz picked up where technical know-how failed Casne. "I could manually throttle injections, I think. Yeah."

"Okay." Casne put her hand on Kalo's shoulder. He bent to accommodate her added weight, and his arm wrapped around her waist. "Get me to that Tiresh, and let's get out of here."

"What do you mean, *let's*?" Kalo objected. Triz stumbled to her feet too, somehow less graceful than Casne despite two functional legs. She felt a stab of guilt over that but pushed it and a reflexive apology aside. Kalo went on, "You're hurt, Cas. Triz and I have got this covered."

"Excuse me, *Lieutenant*?" Casne's eyebrows shot up. "You don't get to give me orders. And I'm not the one who's medically grounded, either."

"Casne, it's okay," Triz cut in. "We don't need you to fly the ship or handle the engine." But the words felt like a lie as soon as they left her mouth. The endless void of space loomed over her, and maybe she didn't need Casne the way she had needed a friend when she stumbled into the bright lights of a new Hab. But, oh yes, she surely did *want* her there. Casne grinned at her, and Triz felt a foolish smile lift her own cheeks in answer.

"We're finishing this together."

* * *

THEY RAN to throw cleaning pods and coolant lines clear of the Tiresh. Kalo slid into the pilot's couch, and Casne buckled herself into the restraints of the forward gunner's rack. Triz settled for the rear gunner's position. With the harness snugly fastened, her legs just barely reached the floor. A swift sweep of her cutting tool opened an impromptu ventral access panel in the grating between her feet. "I'm set here," she called over her shoulder as she pinned a clamp into place to reroute the injection shunt. Another thought occurred to her. "Wait—Kalo, how are you going to fly this thing one-handed?"

"There's a galaxy of distance between one-handed and one-armed." Unbearably smug. Triz rolled her head far to the side to peer at him. He'd ripped the sleeve off his (or rather Triz's) shirt and was tying his drooping hand to one side of the steering yoke. "I can do everything I need to."

"Except finish that knot." Casne took pity on him and helped pull it taut. "Didn't the surgeons put those mods in after the thing with the nerve agents at Urnok? Only *you* could find a way to short out topline exonerves."

"Chance encounter with the business end of a metal recycler. Don't recommend it." Kalo gave the knot a few tentative tugs, then used his good hand to work through a complicated series of hooks, levers, and switches. The Tiresh's engines hummed, one beneath Triz's boots and the other one over her head. "You both ready to do this?"

No, screamed Triz's stomach. "Stop talking and get us out there," she said. She was relieved to hear her voice didn't shake as much as her hands did. She tugged on her heat conversion gloves to hide the trembling as well as protect her from any splatter.

Kalo complied. With the lifttrain's help, the Tiresh

cleared its slab, and the airlock dilated at Kalo's request. The Tiresh eased through, the lifttrain retracted, and Triz stared up through the cockpit plastiglass as the wrenchworks disappeared behind the closing lock. A hiss heralded the air pumps kicking in, but the sound slowly faded as the pumps did their job.

Triz couldn't see the outer lock open, but when the ship maneuvered away from the Hab, the lip of the opening couldn't have been more than inches away from the plastiglass shell over her head. "Shitting stars!" she yelped, but the deepening hum of the engine covered her voice. She cursed and fumbled with her gloves to direct the cannula for manual injection. As she watched, the fat, fluted cylinder of Vivik Hab shrank away. Just behind the Hab, the local star flared like a jewel, eclipsed by the crown of the Arcade. At the Hab's midsection, the pair of whaleships on their umbilici dwindled to marbles, then to nothing at all. Triz swallowed. The Hab was still there, she made herself remember, and it still would be when the Tiresh turned homeward.

"Keep us together back there," Kalo said. She could barely hear him over the engines; had he said *us* or *it*? "I've got visual on that Skimmer. No sign of other ships yet, but we'll see what turns up."

Triz's eyes flicked upward. Or what she thought of as upward, at least, not that such a thing mattered out here. That thought made the stars spin sickeningly. She stuck her sore tongue between her teeth and bit gently to distract herself as she hand-pumped the siphon. The engine's noise receded to a dull groaning.

"That's doing it," Casne called out. "That's great, Triz."

Triz's brain couldn't process a response, so she just nodded, unseen, in the rear couch. Too much work to keep an eye on her jury-rigged bypass—and to remember to breathe with that bottomless black painting the paper-thin plastiglass. She inhaled deeply through her nose until heated air scorched her nostrils. She opened the shunt for another injection just as Kalo shouted, "Coming up on him fast!"

Triz risked a peek over her shoulder and his at the view out in front of the Tiresh. She could see the Scooper now too, dull-battered steel light against the dark background. Even as she watched, it grew in size; the Tiresh was gulping down the space between them. The Scooper's engines barely glowed. Of course, Triz hadn't refueled it yet. No acceleration for Rocan.

But as she stared, a glimmer sparked at the front of the Skimmer, near the cockpit. Something bigger than the far-off stars just beyond, though she couldn't have said what exactly. "What was that?" she said.

Kalo didn't jump at her voice in his ear. "That light? Don't know. Looked almost like he was firing something, but Scoopers aren't equipped with—what is *that*?"

All three of them leaned toward the front plastiglass. Far in front of the Skimmer, no bigger than Triz's thumbnail, a patch of space suddenly shone golden-white. "Son of a Golrosk," said Casne softly. "He's got a tunneler."

Triz frowned. "A tunnel*gun*?"

"No," said Kalo, just as Casne said, "Sort of." Casne went on: "The tech is related, but the tunneler is more complicated. It's a big, temporary stable tunnel to somewhere else. A more predictable somewhere-else than what comes out of a tunnelgun." She cursed. "He was blind in his left eye during that fight. I thought his tech was just on the fritz. If the Ceebees have miniaturized tunneltech that small . . ."

"So he's going to get away?" The Tiresh couldn't intercept in time, even with the Scooper's lazy drift. Triz let herself fall back against her seat. Through the dorsal plastiglass, Vivik hung, familiar but far. Still in sight. At least they could still go back safely . . .

"Not a chance." Kalo reached across his body for a set of controls down on his left side. "Triz, back in position. I'm going to need you to time a double injection. And for all gods' sake, make sure your harness is tight."

She gave the restraints a testing tug even as a scowl crimped her face. "A double shot will just slow us down. I don't see how that's going to help."

"Just buckle up, Triz, before I turn you into a smear on the rear 'glass."

Triz buckled. She also opened her mouth to tell him where to shoot his attitude, just as the Tiresh shuddered hard. Her teeth clacked together, and the shunt jumped out of her hand. She snatched it out of its dead float just before the Tiresh coughed angrily and screamed forward into space. Triz opened the shunt just in time and let the engines guzzle deeply. "You shorted the butterfly valve," she shouted. "Are you crazy? They aren't built for that!"

"Don't. Tell me. How to do. My job."

Triz craned her neck. The Tiresh was closing the distance to the Scooper at an alarming rate now. Kalo was angling to put the gunship between the tunnel and Rocan. Triz hissed and clutched at her restraints as if they would protect her from a mid-space collision.

"Prepare to fire," said Kalo.

"No, Lieutenant." Casne's voice was steel-hard. Strange to hear her sound like a Fleet captain and not an old friend. "Rocan's getting a trial so he can testify in front of all of the

Confederated Worlds what he did. To Hedgehome, to the Golrosk. To me."

Silence from Kalo. They were almost to the Scooper now. Triz wanted to say something and didn't dare interrupt now. "Okay," Kalo said finally. "Proposals?"

"There's a hole in his plastiglass where the tunneler went through." Grim satisfaction from Casne. "The Tiresh has a boarding hook. Vent the cockpit."

Triz squeezed her eyes shut, waiting for Kalo to countermand that insane idea. No pilot alive could hit an angle that precisely, and no one at all could aim their own body at a flying starship at eight hundred klicks an hour. But instead, Kalo said, "Triz, when I tell you, I want you to exhale as hard as you can. Do you understand?"

Her own voice sounded very far away when she heard herself say, "Yes." Casne reached over the couch in front to squeeze her shoulder. Triz clenched her teeth at the sound of restraints releasing.

"I've got control of this fighter. Don't worry." The Tiresh slid into place between the Scooper and the tunnel. A well-timed burst of the upper engine cut their inertia so hard Triz slammed against her restraints.

"It's going to be over soon, Triz." Casne sounded like she believed that. So Triz believed it too. "We did it. *You* did it."

" . . . Okay." The Scooper was so close now. In Triz's head a refrain roared: *she's not really going to do this. She's not* really *going to do this.* Kalo flipped a switch, and billows of frozen white gas erupted from the seams in the plastiglass. They bloomed out of the Tiresh like tiny nebulae. "Tell me when."

Casne pulled a lever and the Tiresh hummed. Over Triz's head, a black cable unspooled. It struck home in the

Scooper, and held fast; another brief spasm from the Tiresh's engine's bruised Triz's ribs. It also broke the Scooper's inertia and held it close in the boarding hook cable's embrace. "All right," Casne said, "we're go in three—two—one—now!"

"*Now*, Triz!"

Triz blew out as hard as she could. Overhead, the plastiglass parted like a breaking window. Casne kicked out from her seat, and the Scooper was still so far away, except that it wasn't at all, was it, and the plastiglass shell closed overhead, and black sparks tore at Triz's vision, she couldn't see to release another injection of coolant, but they'd stopped now anyway, Kalo only needed sub-min engine effort to collect Casne, or was it Triz who was out there, going hand-over-hand between one ship and the next, and what the shitting stars was he yelling at her about now, she just needed a little *rest* . . .

CHAPTER ELEVEN

SOUND RETURNED SLOWLY. Raised voices, what felt like an icy collar pinned around her neck. Triz blinked her eyes open. Her head was pounding, and her mouth tasted like she'd been guzzling rotten algae. "I think I threw up," she said, coughing. Those were Casne's frozen hands on her shoulders, Casne's body squeezed in alongside hers, Casne's laughter in her ears. When she kissed Triz's forehead, her lips left a burning-cold imprint. Triz's head lolled to the other side, where Rocan slouched beside her in the empty gunner's couch. Blood trickled down his face from the space where his eyes should have been, and his left wrist bent inward at a nauseous angle.

"You did it," Triz said.

"Thanks to you," said Casne, still drifting in the space just over Triz's head. "Are you sure you didn't miss your calling not joining the Fleet?"

"We'll get the Admiralty to start a new division." Kalo sounded space-roughened. Triz would feel a little better about her own performance if he'd lost his lunch mid-vent too. "Combat Mechanics. It's catchy."

Triz wanted to tell Casne she should sit down and buckle up like the respectable Fleet officer she was—but found she didn't have it in her. She clutched Casne's bloody, space-cold hand and pressed herself into the shelter of Casne's cold body until it warmed against her. Together they stretched their necks and watched Vivik grow big and bright and blissfully closer on the face of the plastiglass.

BY THE TIME they touched down, the regular lights in the wrenchworks had come back on, albeit not at quite their full intensity. Rocan had also come around, cursing and spitting at Kalo and Casne as they maneuvered him out of the Tiresh. "The Cyberbionautic Alliance will never accede to the hidebound rules of unmodified humanity," he said, as they hauled him up by his elbows and dragged him toward the battered doors of the remaining lift, with Triz leading the way. "Nor will I. I will not stop, nor rest, until your memories are unwound from the fabric of the universe, until your genes unspooled from the common bindings of humankind. Until—"

Triz turned around and struck him in the belly with the flat of her belt wrench.

He gasped for air, staggered, and fell silent. A temporary solution, but sometimes temporary solutions were the best path to someplace more permanent.

"Triz." Casne shook her head.

Triz ignored her and keyed in a lift call.

But she hadn't yet finished when the lift doors shivered

and ground open. The doors parted, and inside stood Quelian, flanked by half a dozen Justice officers.

"Hi, Quelian," Triz said as he stared at her in shock. "Sorry, we kind of made a mess of the 'works."

Before Quelian could ask what happened, his daughter stepped forward and saluted. "Quelian Vivik Orist." Casne's cold formality to her father gave Triz goosebumps. "I stand to remand myself, and Rocan Dustald-3 Melviq of the Cyberbionautic Alliance to the wisdom of Justice."

Triz bit her tongue on an inappropriate comment about the level of wisdom currently on offer there.

At Quelian's nod, the Justice officers moved forward to flank Casne and Rocan. "Put the Ceebee in cryo," Quelian ordered. His gaze fell on his daughter next. "Considering the current state of Justice, Captain Casne is remanded to her usual onhab quarters for the time being." He gave them the location marker of Triz's pairhome. When he finished, he looked as if he would have liked to say something else. Of course, saying things was never Quelian's strong suit. Not saying the *right* things, certainly. He nodded once at Casne, and she returned the gesture in kind. Triz turned away from whatever understated familial communion was happening without her there, and found herself face to face with Kalo.

"Come on, greasemark," he said, and flung his bad arm across her shoulder. "My bootlaces are untied. Carry me out of here while the grownups figure this out."

CHAPTER TWELVE

AFTER NEW EVIDENCE was provided by a pair of Ceebees left for dead by their lord commander in his ill-fated escape from Justice, a missive from Centerpoint waived the necessity for Quelian to recuse himself. The Ceebee lieutenants testified in the circular court at the crown of Justice, raising their voices to speak over the temporary air circulators brought in to work around the damage. A Ceebee agent in the Hab had handed off a biobomb packet to Lanniq. That agent had then fled Vivik for greener Ceebee pastures in the Webward Pearls or farther still. Lanniq was left to plant the packet on the surface of the Hab during one of his training flights. Upon detonation, it had opened a hole in Justice, and the microorganisms hadn't been stopped before they wreaked havoc on the facilities of the Arcade. Every plastic surface had been consumed by the corrosion Triz had seen from the wrenchworks wallport. In Justice, too, there had once been circles of plastiprint benches in the spectator ring. Now, most of the gathered crowd stood. But they stood solemnly, and proudly, to listen as the ashen-faced Ceebees recited their confessions.

A sedate pallor hung over the hearings, absent of the usual theatrics from the Advocates. Four civilians and two Fleet officers had been killed by the Ceebee plot. And then there was Lanniq.

The crowds did not boo or jeer when the Ceebees explained the placement of undetonated missiles in the destroyed Arcology at Hedgehome, as an insurance technique against the expected Fleet reprisal. Only a few angry murmurs cut through as the junior Ceebee officer demonstrated the advanced techniques used to falsify the firing solution Casne had allegedly programmed. Finally, the Ceebee's Advocate instructed them to demonstrate the final component in their confession: the backdoor exploit into Fleet personnel files the Ceebees used to find the best candidates to cause mayhem to the Fleet.

Lanniq had been one such candidate, of course. Originally targeted for his wife's position in Counterintelligence, they'd been able to wield his stray Ceebee nephew as a lever against him. The boy's life in exchange for Rocan's freedom and Casne's honor: a trade he had chosen, however painfully, to make.

And of course, Casne Vivik Veling herself had been a gold mine of a find for them: not only was her father the only high-ranking civilian tribune in the nearest several systems, but they also shared an unstable family psych profile to boot. Casne and Quelian sat, mirror images of stone-faced statues, as the Ceebee witnesses and Justice questioners dissected their relationship. Of course, Casne wasn't the only one who had been affected; two more earlier Interior Watch investigations were set to be reopened immediately based on the new evidence at hand as well.

"Thorough," noted Quelian, who looked odd to Triz in his red Justice robes rather than a stained jumpsuit. She wasn't sure whether he meant the Ceebees' work or that of the questioners. He didn't look at his daughter, who sat just inside the ring of spectators. But her hard, dark eyes bored holes through the fabric over his heart. Triz, forced to watch from the distance of the spectator circle, opened and closed a valve clip from the Tiresh that she still needed to fix, to make her hands forget they weren't holding Casne's. She checked the back of the gallery from time to time, too, but Kalo never did manage to put in an appearance. In fact, Triz hadn't seen him since she deposited him at the medical bay. As if she wasn't worried enough already.

Earlier, in private, the Ceebees had testified about Lanniq, and provided details on the location of his family to be passed on to those in the Fleet who could do something about the situation. His Ceebee nephew was still alive, they swore. The Fleet assured Casne that the young man would be retrieved and returned to his family in due course; that Lanniq had not died for nothing. That loyalty to family over Fleet was not an offense to be paid out in the boy's blood. Triz had heard about that part of the deal only in passing, a few terse words between Casne and her father on the way into the hearing. For now, in public, they kept to the matter at hand, and finally, the three tribunes voted unanimously to void the charges against Casne. Beside Triz, Veling burst into tears, and the other quadparents were unable to contain a gleeful whoop. Casne looked up at the three quadparents, a half-grin splitting her face as the Fleet tribune told her to go join them. She didn't wait for the guard to open the gate around the spectators' ring, but leaped it with a one-handed boost and flung herself into her mother's waiting arms. Triz's face warmed watching them and she turned to go, to let Casne and her family celebrate together.

But Veling caught her sleeve before she could retreat. "Where do you think you're going? This family has a lot of celebrating to catch up on."

Now the warm flush in Triz's cheeks felt close to superheating. Too bad she didn't have a deft mechanic around to manually input some coolant. "I should let you have some time to yourselves," she protested, tugging her arm free of Veling's grasp.

"'To ourselves' is supposed to include you, woman, so stop trying to wriggle out of it. You're not a guttergirl anymore, and we're not a churnpit you have to escape from before it crushes you."

"Aren't we?" said Casne, and picked Triz up in a black hole of a hug. The sensation was not unlike struggling for air in the vented Tiresh cockpit, except warmer and with a much stronger sense of up and down. "Tea at Mirede's. Come on."

"Our treat!" Veling insisted.

The crowd thinned around them, and they started picking their way toward the nearest entrance. But Casne stopped and looked over her shoulder at the empty dais. Triz's hand found her waist, and Casne turned back to her with a small, taut smile. "I'll tell you what, Mama," she said. "You and Dad and Damu go on ahead. We'll meet you there in a little while."

Veling's hands stretched out to squeeze one of Casne's shoulders and one of Triz's. "We're a family, you know that, don't you? All of us, and you. Nantha too. Whatever he does or says. With or without him."

"I know it," said Casne, and Veling let them go. It was only after they'd parted way from the others that Casne leaned in to Triz's ear and said, "And I'm going to do a better job of making sure *you* know it."

By the time they arrived in the wrenchworks, Casne looked a bit more rumpled in her dress greens than would have passed Fleet codes, and Triz was sweating. She combed her hair back into her braid with one finger and looked around the works. "Quelian? You down here?"

A moment of silence, and Triz thought she'd guessed wrong. Before she could turn back to Casne, a balding head poked out of the office door. "What do you want?"

Casne's strength and solidity behind her shoulder made her feel brave: not the superficial sort of brave that warded off problems with a cutting quip, but something more enduring. She could understand, briefly and piercingly, how much it must have hurt when Quelian had that pillar pulled out from under the ceiling of his life plans. It didn't excuse what he'd done or who he'd become in the meantime. But she understood it. She understood it to an uncomfortable extent. "Quelian," Triz said, "come up to Mirede's and have tea and dinner with your family before you lose them." An indrawn breath from Casne behind her and Triz quickly amended: "Before you lose *us*."

Quelian huffed something like a laugh as he emerged from the office and crammed his discarded Justice wrap into a half-open locker. His jumpsuit was relatively clean, the sleeves still rolled down. "I lost the lot of you the day this one sailed off to the academy."

"That's the way you cast it for yourself. So you came out

the tragic hero of the wrenchworks." Casne spoke levelly, but Triz could feel the tension as each word snapped short between her teeth. "Poor Quelian. No one else understands how hard he has it. Me hitting the eject button out of here as a traitor, which, of course, made Mama and Dad and Damu collaborators." Her hand found Triz's waist and tightened. "And Triz here to take the place you'd made for me. You could never quite figure out whether or not you were glad of that. If the wound didn't heal right, Quelian, it's because you never stopped picking at it."

Quelian didn't answer, just crossed the works to one of the Skimmers. "We're behind as it is. The Fleet's penny-pinchers aren't going to give two shits if the Hab's had a hole blown in the side of it when it comes to pay." He paused with a tension spanner raised halfway to the Skimmer's hull. "I'd need another sure hand with a laser drill to help me catch up in time."

That was an offer of her job back, if she wasn't mistaken, in Quelian's oblique way. Probably the most effort at an apology she'd see. She wasn't sure it was enough of one. But it was somewhere to start. And life on the Hab wouldn't be the same without her job. "Come uphab," she said. "Everyone will be waiting."

"I will," Quelian said, and worked the spanner into position. "Just need to get an hour of work done. Get a batch of plastisteel curing. Keep things moving along."

"I'd like you to be there, Baba," Casne said, and the spanner froze for just a moment.

Then Quelian nodded. The spanner moved again. "I will," he said, and this time his voice was thick.

Triz put her hand on Casne's shoulder, and they moved back toward the lift. There was no hasty embrace this time, only Casne leaning her head to the side to rest it atop Triz's as the lift mechanism whirred gently outside. Maybe Quelian would come and maybe he wouldn't. Up to him, now. And up to them not to let him spoil the day in any case. There would be time to work over the engine of that relationship. And to consign it to the recycler if necessary, too. Triz could still work in the wrenchworks without having to particularly enjoy sharing it with Quelian. But she hoped that wouldn't be the case.

The lift exhaled them onto the lowest level of the Arcade, and Triz wished Mirede's tearoom lay just a little closer to the lift depot because it seemed like everyone on the Hab wanted to stop to greet Casne and congratulate her along the way. They were close enough to the tearoom doors for Triz to peep inside when they were waylaid once more—but this time, the would-be accoster grabbed both of their sleeves to spin them around.

"Kalo!" Casne exclaimed, and shoved his shoulder. "Where were you earlier? It's not like you to wait to show up till all the drama's over."

"All due congratulations to my favorite ex-convict. It's good to see you on the right side of Justice." He pressed a kiss to Casne's lips, then pulled back with a grin. "But I had a date that couldn't be missed. With the technosurgeon." He waved the fingers of his left hand, then further demonstrated their restored function by making a gesture that would have gotten him roughed up in at least three Habs and possibly arrested in another. "Happy to report all systems are back online. Which reminds me, now I'm able to do this . . ." He locked his fingers around Triz's wrist and pulled her in close. "Triz Rydoine Cierrond. By the authority of Admiral Savelian Dustald-4 Edantha—"

"What?"

"—I hereby and thusly bestow upon thou the Doing Great Stuff Commendation for Valor Under Extremely Terrible Circumstances." He pinned a small silver medal to the breast pocket of her jacket. When he let it drop down onto the coarse fabric, it didn't quite manage to conceal a large grease stain. Kalo nodded in satisfaction as Triz canted her head forward to peer at it.

"It's the Alchemy Medal," said Casne, leaning forward for a better look. "That's the second-highest civilian commendation the Fleet gives out."

"Really?" Triz tapped the metal with one fingernail, liking the little ping it made. "Shitting stars. What does someone have to do to get the highest one?"

Kalo turned to Casne. "Afraid I haven't got anything for you. You know the Admiral's insisting on pinning one on you himself, the whole ceremony deal. Dress blacks. Speeches. Drummers, probably." He cackled. "Oh gods! I bet they'll make you do the Fleet Prayer in front of everyone."

A strained noise escaped from Casne. "Can't I just do another unplanned space swim instead? It would probably be more fun."

"Hey, I'm going to have to be there too. We'll suffer side by side. And speaking of fun." Kalo jerked a shoulder at the tearoom. "I think you've got a party waiting for its guest of honor in there."

"I know!" Casne straightened up from another inspection of Triz's medal. "We just keep getting delayed by the worst kinds of people. Are you joining us?"

"Me? Oh, no, I'll get out of the way. Just let me borrow Triz for a minute, will you?"

Casne raised her eyebrows, but shrugged and stepped away. "As long as I see you soon."

Triz pursed her lips. Now she stood alone with Kalo, her back against the tearoom wall and no place to hide except behind a sarcastic comment. "I feel like if you're going to ask about borrowing me, I should be the first person you put the question to?"

"But I'm not borrowing you from yourself. You're still here, aren't you? It's only Cas that I'm depriving of your company for my own selfish purposes." He sidled around beside her, leaning against the hastily painted metal that constituted Mirede's storefront until proper repairs were finished. She recognized what he was doing: offering an escape route besides the one through him. "You know how Vivik is sort of a shipping hub? Scooper dumps and big freighters come through here all the time."

She couldn't quite contain an eye-roll. "Wow, Kalo, is it really? Do you think maybe that's why I spend so much time neck-deep in Scoopers and lugs in the wrenchworks?"

He shoved his hands in his pockets and kept talking, ignoring her. "Apparently there's been a little pirate traffic in some of the Outward lanes lately. Fleet's signing pilots over to operate out of Sidorrey and run escorts where they're needed."

"Sidorrey's not far from here," Triz observed. Her tongue clung to the roof of her mouth and turned the S of "Sidorrey" into a sticky "guh". Picking off the occasional pirate would be a safer docket than clearing out the remainder of the Ceebee nests pocketed across the Confederated worlds. "Is that what you're—I mean, is that what you want to do?"

"What I want is to keep flying." Kalo's fingers drummed

on his thigh. "Don't know if they'll take a recruit who's got a history of turning his fighter into a shrapnel collector, and even if they did, it would be half a dozen cycles before the paperwork even gets pushed through. And if the Fleet flushes out another Ceebee cache, I'd go back in. That's not something I can just walk away from. No one should." He hastily added, "And I won't put in for it at all if it's not something you're interested in. I just thought, things being what they are . . . I'm not asking you to form a gon with me, or with me and Casne and Nan, or at all. But if you wanted to take a test flight on what it would be like . . ."

Triz's stomach roiled with confusion. "That would put you farther from Casne. And if you're not stationed with a whale, you won't get to Centerpoint to see Nantha as often, either."

"That's not—" He exhaled noisily. "Gods of Issam, do I have to write it down for you? Casne and Nan too, they're some of my best friends and I love them dearly. Sometimes I'm half-sure they even like me. But I wanted, uh. Not just them. A partner. A gon doesn't work when it's two people and a diagonal line. You know?"

"No! Why would you—" She felt his arm stiffen against hers. Her mind flicked through a stack of discarded images: the night when Casne introduced them and the stab of relief she'd felt when he first smiled at her to show off those crooked teeth. Ribbondancing in the nullgrav disco and screaming with laughter like giddy children. Kalo's greasy boots on the sofa in her rooms, and his stupid hair falling across his stupid face while he slept. Watching that 'port footage of dying Fleet ships and their terrible fight afterward. The ugly words she'd said and never got around to apologizing for. Maybe she was more

Quelian's daughter than either of them had ever managed to believe.

No, she had time.

She would find a way yet. "I mean. I think so. Maybe. Yes."

His eyebrows curved upward in confusion. "So . . . I should . . ."

"Put in for the transfer." She put her hand in his. The same size as Casne's, but cooler to the touch. Familiar and strange. "Yes. Shit. I'm going to have to get used to seeing your face around, I guess."

"Talk to the technosurgeon," he suggested, "they might be able to get you some anti-nausea drugs that'll help." He shoved her shoulder, making her double-step away from the wall. "Now go party before the next shitting tragedy takes a bite out of this Hab."

She leaned toward him. If she kissed him now, the wave function would collapse, and this would all come apart. "I'll see you later?"

"I know where you live," he said, and those words held so much weight she could've pinned it to her chest in place of her medal and worn it just as proudly.

TRIZ'S ALARM BUZZED. "OFF," she said thickly, but of course, she'd programmed the wallport alarm to answer only to her proffered fob and not her voice, to make sure she actually got out of bed. It wasn't as if she even had a job to get up for anymore—oh. Right. She sat up.

The bed in her rooms was *absolutely* not big enough for three, though that was how many people it had held tangled together in the comfortable closeness of half-sleep (and before that, not-sleep) for the night. "I should get up," Casne muttered without moving. She occupied the sliver of mattress between Triz and the floor; one of her arms hung over the side. Maybe Triz should apply for something bigger than the pairhome. Well, she didn't have to worry about that today.

"Don't you know we're on leave?" Kalo sprawled on the other side of her, legs twisted into well-kicked sheets. "Or don't you care? Some things are sacred." He put a pillow over his head. "Which reminds me. Triz, go shut up your alarm."

"You should be grateful." Triz slithered out between their two bodies and slid to the foot of the bed, where she stretched her cramped shoulders. "It's telling me to get up and fix a shitload of Light Attack Craft today."

A hand slid around her waist and between her thighs. She spread her legs wider. Shitting alarm. "Just don't stay at work too long," said Kalo into the skin of her back. "We'll be here. Alone. Bored. Too lazy to get up. Practically wasting away."

"You'll be fine." With a pang of regret, Triz stood and tossed the wadded-up sheets back down on him. He sputtered and flopped back down. "I hear you've got two functional hands now."

"I should get up," Casne said again, as if trying to convince herself of this.

Triz leaned over to kiss Cas' forehead. "The Hero of Golros gets to lie abed as long as she shitting wants." Casne's nose wrinkled into a smile; Triz pressed a warm, wet kiss to her lips where they parted. Then she straightened up and stretched. She really did have to go to work. Yesterday's jumpsuit lay on the floor; she pulled it up her legs and suggested, "And if you need more room in bed, just shove Kalo on the floor."

"You're a cruel woman!" he called after her as she staggered sleepily toward the bathroom. "In fact, I plan to stay here in bed all day plotting my revenge."

"As long as you're both here," she said, and closed the door between them before she could embarrass either of them more with overfondness.

GLOSSARY

A

22CR Starbusters: A slightly outdated but entirely deadly model of large-payload missiles.

Admiral Savelian Dustald-4 Edantha: Senior Fleet officer in the sector; credited with the successful Fleet campaign against Cyberbionautic forces.

Advocate: A speaker for the affected party, in legal matters and negotiations, assigned by Public Welfare.

Aerobacter: One of several oxygenic bacteria species modified for symbiotic use in human beings, particularly those operating in deep space or deep water.

Alchemists: An outdated class of Light Attack Craft legendary for their inability to take a hit.

Alchemy Medal: The second-highest honor bestowed by the Fleet on civilians; given in recognition of the recipient's conversion of certain defeat into victory.

Allibek's Wings: A Fleet honor bestowed in recognition of outstanding valor in the face of overwhelming odds.

Andeus: A dwarf planet in the Coreward region, known primarily for its exports of ore and aspiring Fleet officers.

Arcade: A common area found in most space habitats, as well as on each level of any planned planetary colonies built by the Confederated Worlds.

Arcology: A planet-based enclosed artificial habitat.

Arcwing: A class of Light Attack Craft built for sturdiness over speed and featuring heavier artillery than Skimmer models.

Armward Bands: Densely-populated clusters of Confederated Worlds habitats and planetary structures along the arm of the spiral galaxy.

Artigrav: Shorthand for artificial gravity, especially for mechanics who might have to say those words a lot.

Astral Noise: The latest and greatest band to hit the

Confederated Worlds, as long as you're a fan of screamwave splatterpop.

Auzhni Hab: A small Hab based near the Hedgehome system.

B

Biobomb: Pairs an explosive device with an engineered microorganism for maximum damage. A typical use case might include an infectious bacterium, or, when deployed against infrastructure, microbes that corrode plastic or specific types of metal.

Biolights: Emergency temporary bioluminescence; a habitat or Arcology's power failure triggers the release of substrate that feeds dormant microorganisms and induces luminescence.

Biomods: Shorthand for biological modifications, ranging from symbiotic bacteria to cybernetic limb replacement.

Birdflute: A high-pitched wind instrument that sounds like beautiful birdsong in the hands of an expert player, or, with less skillful use, a dying parakeet.

C

Ceebee: Shorthand for a member of the Cyberbionautic Alliance.

Centerpoint Station: The primary base of operations for the Confederated Fleet. Originally established at roughly the center of the settled Confederated Worlds; not so much anymore, but two prior attempts to rename it have failed due to linguistic inertia.

CFS Graithe: A Confederated Fleet cruiser lost with all hands in a battle with Cyberbionautic forces, trying unsuccessfully to buy time for the CFS Iuelo, her sister ship, to escape.

Chimon: Site of a minor skirmish between Confederated Fleet and Cyberbionautic forces; considered the last real engagement of the war.

Churnpit: Another name for a recycling engine, particularly a poorly maintained one.

Cierrond: An elderly Tolvian mendicant who was of Triz's earliest teachers and one of the few as stubborn as she was; Triz took his name as her parent name when he died.

Clusterward: The region of a large cluster of stars, mostly unpopulated, located between the human-inhabited arm of the Galaxy and the largely unexplored arm on the opposite side.

Commander Escoth: Strategy Division Lead for the Confederated Fleet; the grandson of luxury starship magnate Idri Croelo Escoth.

Commander Rocan Dustald-3 Melviq of the Cyber-

bionautic Alliance, the Unquenchable Scythe: A much higher name-to-person ratio than is ever justifiable.

Confederated Fleet: A military force devoted to protecting the safety and wellbeing of the member planets and habitats of the Confederated Worlds.

Confederated Worlds: A loose alliance of several hundred human settlements. The first Habs were admitted 137 Standard Cycles ago after pressure from several outlying systems to broaden the definition of what constituted a "world".

Croelo Hab: A large Hab in the Armward Bands and one considered, especially by the outlying planets and Habs, to be the height of style.

Cyberbionautic Alliance: A quasi-political separatist entity led by Rocan Dustald-3 Melviq, which holds modified bodies as superior to unmodified and believes that, as they shape their bodies to fit their environment, their environment should meet them halfway—regardless of who may already be living quite comfortably in it.

D

Dailos: Flagship of Admiral Savelian's First Wing of the Confederated Fleet; the ship where Casne, Kalo, Saabe, and Lanniq serve.

Damu: A common nickname for nonbinary parents; most

often used by children but retained into adulthood by some, especially doting offspring.

Darts: An outdated class of Light Attack Craft legendary for their inability to take a hit.

Distribution Council: The governing body in charge of managing public assets in Vivik Hab and some other similarly-run Habs.

Do-Ffash: An extended family of pirates operating primarily out of the Webward Pearls.

Dry-pearls: A semi-precious gem produced in what could broadly be called the "stomach" of a sedentary creature called a stillmouse, native to, and only found on, the planet Erret.

E

Edillo: The original owner, presumably, of the Vivik Hab establishment known as Edillo's. Early Distribution Council records are spotty, and no one actually remembers anyone named Edillo.

Erret: An apparent desert world to the naked eye, with a rich and almost entirely subterranean water supply and native biota.

Erron: A fairly recent planetary establishment; only two levels of the Arcology have yet been built.

Escoth V-27: A sleek, sporty craft designed for personal travel, for people with more money and leisure time than Triz.

Eusociality: In the spirit of mutual survival, health, and happiness; the ideal to which Vivik Hab's Distribution Council aspires.

Exonerves: An exogenous electrochemical structure replicating the function of the peripheral nervous system; commonly replace damaged nerves in people with certain degenerative diseases as well as hopped-up flyboys with no sense of self-preservation.

Exotics-wranglers: Engineers devoted to developing scalable, reliable Fleet technology based on quantum effects; probably the biggest geeks in the galaxy.

F

Fleet: The Confederated Fleet, the military body organized around the defense of the Confederated Worlds and, more recently, the protection of worlds that harbor alien intelligences.

Fleet Admiralty: The leadership of the Confederated Fleet.

Fleet Counsel: A member of the Fleet's legal organization, assigned to defend Fleet officers accused of any misdoings that fall under Fleet jurisdiction.

Fleet Prayer: A rote prayer invoking the protection of the Gods of Issam and several other accessory deities; written by an officer in time immemorial; recitation takes twelve minutes, and is inflicted daily on Academy enrollees, as well as those unfortunate enough to receive a high-level commendation in the course of duty.

Fleet Standard Time: Based on five cycles of five hours each; the standard clock by which all Fleet vessels operate in order to maintain cohesion across their Galaxy-wide deployment.

Fourth Wing: An entire wing of Fleet ships that defected from duty and disappeared, mostly to parts unknown. The subject of a great deal of speculation wherever two or more Fleet officers and an alcoholic beverage are co-located.

G

Galactic Web: A network of populated worlds and Habs, nearly all of which count themselves as members of the Confederated Worlds.

Ganit's Pantry: A beloved drinking establishment on Vivik Hab, albeit one that takes full advantage surge pricing on its menu.

Gnosseo: Not a member planet of the Confederated Worlds; considers itself highly civilized, which it probably is as long as you have a lot of money and a couple of well-armed bodyguards.

Golros: The home planet of an alien intelligence, the target of Ceebee shotgun-style terraforming, and the location of the battle that made a name for Casne Vivik Veling.

Gonmate: One of two or more members of a platonic, romantic, and/or sexual relationship, around which most households are built.

Greasehead: Nickname bestowed (affectionately?) on certain mechanics, especially by those who have opted into less greasy professions.

Greenwork: The cultivation and upkeep of oxygen-generating algae and other microbiota, required for the preservation of human life in space but which smell like a tree shat itself to death.

Guttergirl: A deprecating term for the unfortunates who are forced to survive on recycling pit scraps by the uncaring Hab where they live.

Gyrax: A type of bomber by the Fleet, mostly deprecated but with a few still lingering on in service.

H

Hab: A Habitation Environment; a space station where human beings reside, many serving as waystations between farflung inhabited worlds.

Hask: Nantha's home base, not far from Centerpoint.

Hedgehome: A populous system with a large Arcology and two nearby Habs, all of which were destroyed in the fighting between the Confederated Fleet and the Cyberbionautic Alliance.

Heliodrome: A banked arena for exercise. Where space jocks go to get their sports on.

Hideslug: A nonsentient cultivated for the production of fine leather goods; happens to look like a legless cow got sucked halfway into a wormhole and then spat back out inside out.

I

Interior Watch: The branch of the Fleet tasked with enforcement of its own internal rules and regulations.

Issam: The Sanctuary World, said to be the first settled after humanity left its forgotten home planet; makes a good story, anyway.

Iuelo: A CFS ship lost with all hands in spite of the valiant efforts of her sister ship, the CFS Graithe, to buy time for her escape.

J

Justice: An important social role in Confederated World arcologies and Habs, the members of which work to adjudicate disputes and legal proceedings and to ensure that Distribution proceeds fairly among all members of the local population. The success of these efforts is highly relative depending on the Hab in question.

L

Light Attack Craft: The varied assortment of fighters, bombers, and other small, more-or-less maneuverable vessels attached to the Fleet.

Lithogrunge: A percussion-heavy, bass-dense, lowkey musical style; great for kidney stones.

M

Mealcase: A personalized serving size of the Hab meal being distributed for any given meal.

Metal Reclamation: A typical Hab facility; waste not, want not, especially when the hull needs patching.

Mirede: Proprietor of a tearoom on Vivik Hab and a very pleasant busybody.

N

Nav: Shorthand for Navigation, often used by people too busy making Navigation calculations to say the whole word.

Nullgrav: A zero-gravity recreation environment; waivers required.

P

Pairhome: Hab-allocated housing optimally sized to a two-person pair, with or without children.

Parallax: A heavily-armored Fleet advance ship meant to draw fire from enemy forces (and withstand it).

Photosnap: Like a selfie, but in space!

Plastiglass: A synthetic, durable glass substitute that patches itself on impact, a highly desirable quality if you want to have windows and also breathe in space.

Plastiprint: Synthetic plastic-based fabrication printed to specification: mealcases, benches, accessories, and more. Please recycle.

Plastisteel: A very strong synthetic metal substitute with steel-like durability and plastic-like mass.

Portlounge: A small area in many living quarters based around the port, the source of news, music, and entertainment. Smaller Habs or arcologies may have a single larger portlounge where families can gather.

PubWel: Public Welfare; the elected representatives responsible for enacting policies to uphold eusocial ideals, safety, and equity in the Hab.

Q

Quadborn: A child born to any member or members of a particular quadfamily. In a healthy quad, a child born to any member is treated as the child of all members, though most children are aware of who their biological parent or parents in the quad are.

Quadfamily: A family unit based around a four-person platonic, romantic, and/or sexual relationship, with or without children.

Quadhome: Hab-allocated housing optimally sized to a four-person quad, with or without children.

R

Recycling Engine: A massive composting container for organic waste generated by a Hab or Arcology; generates fertilizer for the environment's Terraria and mushroom farms; the warmth generated is often used to heat adjacent housing.

Roia: The minimally-settled planet that houses a number of nonsentient species, including the Roian hideslug, and the type of humans who don't mind or even enjoy living in an environment that is actively trying to murder them all the time.

Rydoine: The type of Hab where Justice's attentions are not entirely evenly distributed; Triz's Hab of origin.

S

Sanishar: The site of a newly discovered extinct alien-intelligence civilization; exciting stuff if you're into it.

Scalecloth: A decorative fabric hand-sewn with the scales of Emperor Lizards native to Roia. Emperor Lizards are neither emperors nor technically lizards; they are, however, sparkly.

Scooper: An ore-mining vessel employed in asteroid mines. Slow, sturdy, and reliable.

Sei Worldhold: A system of three planetary systems and one Hab located just outside the fringes of the Confederated Worlds. A strongly hierarchical society; though their relations with the Confederated Worlds are friendly, both sides are rather bewildered by the other.

Seventh God of Issam: Patron deity of Navigators and engineers; avatar of human ingenuity; a holy math nerd.

Sidorrey: A small Fleet-operated Hab located not far from Vivik. Organized around preventing and intercepting piracy.

Simek green wine: An unusual vintage originating in the Armward Bands; a typical drink order for a nervous recluse trying to look at least a little sophisticated.

Skimmer: A speedy and highly maneuverable variety of Light Attack Craft; the preferred starfighter of those who like to live fast, die young, and leave an incinerated corpse.

Starslicers: A vintage model of Light Attack Craft; named by someone with a lot more enthusiasm than their janky handling and ugly fuselage warrants.

Sugarpips: The seeds of a particular fruit; a delicacy whose subtle flavors are difficult to perfectly capture via food printer, except perhaps to the undiscerning palate of a kid who grew up eating garbage for breakfast.

Swalen: The Third God of Issam; a jock, brawler, and all around good-time girl who would probably be delighted to find that her name was regularly invoked as profanity.

T

Technosurgeon: A medical professional trained in both human anatomy and physiology and exogenous implant technology.

Terraria: An area of Habs and arcologies built around green plants and trees; supplies oxygen, fresh fruits and vegetables, and a bit of mental health.

The Cosset: A Vivik Hab venue for upscale sex work; the most famous on the Hab and also the most expensive. The locals tend to choose other establishments.

Tiresh: A four-person gunship that under no circumstances should be flown with a misfiring injector.

Tolvian: Mendicant monks and far-travelers, followers of the philosopher-poet Tolvia, devoted to her creed of lifting up the least and lowest in the Galaxy.

Tunnelgun: A quantum-effects-based weapon that can cut through any material by, on a fundamental physical level, convincing the atoms involved that they simply do not exist.

Tunneltech: The hardware involved in the deployment of a tunnelgun.

U

Upclass: Fancy; elegant; perhaps even snooty.

Uphab: Habs with artificial gravity enjoy perpetuating the notions of "up" and "down"; uphab levels are those at the imaginary top, downhab at the imaginary bottom.

Urnok: An unaffiliated Hab: unaffiliated with any major governments, trade organizations, or indeed laws.

W

Webward Pearls: A string of several unaffiliated planets, most of which don't mind housing pirate swarms (some of which function as essential privateers on behalf of Pearl-based interests), nor Ceebee fleets as well as broader human supremacy movements.

Whaleships: The biggest ships in the Confederated Fleet, which house Light Attack Swarms, heavy artillery, and a great deal of officers. Built to take a hit. Built to take *several.*

Wrenchworks: A ship repair and general mechanic facility located on any Hab and in some arcologies as well.

Wristfob: A communication, scheduling, and technology-interface device typically worn on the wrist.

ACKNOWLEDGMENTS

Sometimes books just want to have fun. It's amazing how liberating (I won't say easy, because writing is never quite *easy*) it can be to let loose and write the book that just wants to be a big queer happy space romp—not to mention discovering that other people want in on that party, too. I'm so grateful to the wonderful team at Interstellar Flight Press, editor extraordinaire Holly Lyn Walrath and Michael Glazner, for embarking on this trip with me and for doing the hard work of providing a flight map along the way.

There have been so many people who helped with reads and critiques along the way, including the wonderful Codexians (go team BB-8!) who read the first draft; my VP22 classmates Alice Towey and Kaitlyn Zivanovich, who helped me wade through rewrites; Julia Patt, and of course the splendid Bennett North, who is a thoughtful external editor as well as a reliable voice reminding me when to turn off the internal one.

I also owe big thanks to the proofreading crew at Interstellar Flight Press—Joanna Velez, Kaylee Craig, Jeremy Brett, and Corey J. White—who had a mighty big job text-wrangling the kind of messy . . . er, *sprawling* world-building that I tend to generate on the fly, and to cover artist Oleg Tsoy for a fun wrapper that I hope will catch the eye of anyone judging this book by its cover.

And finally, thank you to Mr. Shakespeare, who I think would not object to a remix of this nature: thanks for these dollies to play with! It was a lot of fun to dress them up in space suits and fling them around for a bit.

ABOUT THE AUTHOR

Aimee Ogden is a former science teacher and software tester; now she writes stories about sad astronauts, angry princesses, and dead gods. Her short fiction has appeared in venues such as Analog, Beneath Ceaseless Skies, and Fireside, and another novella, *Sun-daughters, Sea-daughters* is forthcoming from Tor.com. She also co-edits *Translunar Travelers Lounge,* a magazine of fun and optimistic speculative fiction. Find her online at aimeeogdenwrites.wordpress.com.

ABOUT THE COVER ARTIST

Oleg Tsoy is a freelance 2D illustrator, comics artist, and gamer from Almaty, Kazakhstan. His work appears in Russian and Ukrainian comics and magazines. Find him online at Artstation or on Instagram as MasterOfSpirits.

INTERSTELLAR FLIGHT PRESS

Interstellar Flight Press is an indie speculative publishing house. We feature innovative works from the best new writers in science fiction and fantasy. In the words of Ursula K. Le Guin, we need "writers who can see alternatives to how we live now, can see through our fear-stricken society and its obsessive technologies to other ways of being, and even imagine real grounds for hope."

Find us online at www.interstellarflightpress.com.

facebook.com/interstellarflightpress
twitter.com/intflightpress
instagram.com/interstellarflightpress

NEW RELEASES FROM INTERSTELLAR FLIGHT PRESS

The Manticore's Vow by Cassandra Rose Clarke

A vain assassin takes an assignment with dire consequences. An aristocratic lady fleeing her past is besieged by pirates. And a manticore princess sets out on a life-changing adventure.

Interstellar Flight Magazine Best of Year One

From space opera to weird fiction to indie games and NaNoWriMo, this collection represents the best in nonfiction dedicated to geekery. Founded by Holly Lyn Walrath, Interstellar Flight Magazine is an online SFF and pop culture mag devoted to essays on what's new in the world of speculative genres. With interviews, personal essays, rants, and raves, the authors of Interstellar Flight Magazine explore the vast outreaches of nerdom.

Twelve by Andrea Blythe

Twelve is a poetic retelling of the Brothers Grimm fairytale "The Twelve Dancing Princesses." Bewitching and beguiling, this short series of linked poems takes the reader to the underground realm and back, following the stories of twelve princesses and their life after the magic shoes.

CPSIA information can be obtained
at www.ICGtesting.com
Printed in the USA
LVHW020438090721
692195LV00011B/1391

9 781953 736024